a novel

By Michelle Josette

To Kayla-
With much xoxo,
Michelle Josette

Cover design by Clarissa Yeo

ISBN-13: 978-1502447760

ISBN-10: 1502447762

www.mjbookeditor.com

facebook.com/mjbookeditor

MICHELLE JOSETTE

For my sister.

A NOTE FROM THE AUTHOR

Like the rest of the nation, at just fourteen years old I was struck by the horror of 9/11. My world shook; it had been the first big tragedy in my lifetime. My intrigue about what it must have been like for the survivors, victims and their loved ones, combined with my passion for stories about lost love and the human condition, led me to pen my first novel, *After Henry*. It is meant, not to exploit the events of 9/11, but to explore how the human spirit might survive after America's worst tragedy.

PROLOGUE

Sunshine spills into Manhattan. The breeze is calming, swirling around the growing crowd, sending down the first prickly chills of autumn. I wrap my sweater tighter around me and pull the knot of my scarf to my neck as I look past the bronze parapets, where deep scars once pockmarked the location of Ground Zero. Now, blankets of water tumble into pools beneath the surface. *Reflecting Absence*, they're called. It's the reason we've come. To reflect upon the absence.

My name is Emma Jenkins. I stand between two of the greatest remaining loves of my life as we walk the tree-lined perimeter of the pools, stopping to gaze at the flag that hangs from a building above us. I peek over the edge, into the water that gathers before spilling over. There, a young face looks back at me. Green eyes, pale skin. Thick fistfuls of wavy auburn hair. A tiny hand slips into mine, and I squeeze it gently. This is where our story began, and this is where it begins again.

Today marks the tenth anniversary of that day in September—the day I lost my father, my faith, the comfort of my youth. I'd lost the memories, too. Where I'd been, how it had happened. I'd even forgotten who it was who delivered the news to me, and how I had reacted upon hearing it. Did I scream? Cry? Refuse to believe it? Or was that the moment the world had darkened, the moment I simply erased it all?

But I remember it now. I remember the night before, the reason I was here that day. I remember waking up in the hospital, lost in confusion, still barely able to breathe, with the glow of lights and blurry faces over me and the TV as it blared, spouting words I wasn't quite able to comprehend. Yes, I remember now. I remember everything.

Faintly, over the murmur of people and the water that pours, I hear a whisper from behind me, interrupting my thoughts.

"We don't have to stay if you don't want to."

I remind her that it's been ten years already, but she knows the pain isn't gone, though it has certainly dulled. She wouldn't know as well, though; Lois was very young when it happened. She has few memories of our father, and fewer of his death.

Then, for several moments, a stretch of silence opens up between us until I say what I know we've both been thinking: "Mother would have wanted to be here too."

She nods, then I nod, and I take a deep breath, choking back a flood of tears. Our hands come together like magnets.

"Just let me know when you're ready," she says. "We can go anywhere else in the City today."

Anywhere else? I imagine our old childhood home on the Upper East Side. I picture our bedrooms, remembering how

6

Dad would tuck us in. His whiskers that tickled against our chins; the sheets that billowed above our faces; the sound of Mom's laughter in the doorway.

I think of the high school I had attended, the friends I made and lost. I think of the man I loved. His name was Henry, too—like my father. I was like my mother in that way and in that way only. We both had a Henry to love us. We both had a Henry to save us, and a Henry who would ruin us as well.

I remember the moment I saw him again. *My* Henry. It was three years on, early in the fall of 2004, and I had just returned to the City. I was a mess. Still reeling from my father's death three years earlier—my father's and, more recently, my mother's—and with just the smallest glimmer of hope for my future, I had little left to cling to. A silent home, a familiar town. Some old ballet shoes.

I carried with me, too, on my return, a bucket of grief that hadn't quite spilled over, not because it couldn't, but because I hadn't allowed it to. Not yet. I wanted it to freeze instead, so I could hold on to the solid block of it forever. My grief. My heavy, comforting grief, the steady weight of which alone had reminded me that I was, in fact, alive.

The sun hides, and the sky is now covered by a sheet of gray. A flock of birds flies noisily by. The wind blows, slapping a chain against a flagpole in the distance. I inhale deeply again as sticky little fingers wrap tighter around mine, his small mouth opening wide as I lift him up. I watch as he looks at the water below. How much deeper must it seem for him? I think of the places I'll show him today, the things I'll try to explain.

The music begins to play, and the crowd thickens. I trace my father's name, engraved in the cold, dark stone, with my finger. Others bend over to kiss the names of their loved ones, their tears gathering in the crevices of the letters. I don't cry, not today, but manage a smile and grip my sister's hand more firmly. I tell her there's no place I'd rather be than here, today, with the two of them.

MICHELLE JOSETTE

PART ONE

CHAPTER 1

When Emma dances, she knows that what has just been created has flowed through her, from deep within, captivating her audience—even if only the trees that bow against the gentle wind. She is merely witness to its majesty. Its gift to her, if she's lucky, is she gets to lightly touch it on its way through.

Her story begins, for all intents and purposes, early in the fall of 2004 at her grandmother's house in Tillamook, Oregon. Emma Jenkins woke up on the damp porch with the smell of coffee wafting toward her. Not the sweet-smelling flavored coffees and fancy cappuccinos she knew her housemates would have preferred—including her little sister, Lois. She thought it strange at first, Lois drinking coffee (Lois was only ten at the time) but Augusta insisted she'd filled her cup with mostly chocolate. Just a drop of magic. Emma smiled as she poured herself a cup of the dark, thick, oily French roast that must have been made just for her.

She returned to the porch, cradling the mug as she held it to her lips, a blanket wrapped loosely around her, long hair pulled back. The house and farm were eerily quiet. A thin breeze whispered by, chilling her skin, and the clouds had begun to rumble again. Emma looked up from her coffee at the sky above, waiting expectantly for the rain, fully intending to stay outside.

The farm was small and almost completely useless were it not for the chicken coop on the side of the house. She never imagined she'd live in a house with a chicken coop, having grown up in a four-story home on the Upper East Side of Manhattan, but her grandmother, Augusta, was adamant. And she let them choose everything, to really make it theirs. The supplies they needed to build the coop. The paint and flowers and other embellishments to make it pretty for their three new hens. (They named them Emma, Lois, and Augusta—a spark of brilliant creativity, they'd thought.) The girls watched them grow from little chicks, providing them food and shelter and love, caring for them as more than egg-layers, but as pets.

Emma smiled, thinking of the day the first one finally laid an egg. She had been standing in the kitchen with Augusta, stirring a pot of vegetable soup (they'd refused to eat chicken since the arrival of the hens), and Lois came storming in, her face beaming.

"Lois laid an egg! Lois laid an egg!" It was as if Emma's sister had actually done it herself.

Augusta slapped her hands together and smiled. "Well, let's go see it then." Emma abandoned her stirring and hurried out with them, the excitement taking her by surprise.

It was a tiny beige egg, rounded but not quite perfectly round, with a few little dark splotches. Augusta held it out for the girls to see. "It's perfect," she said. Emma shrugged, taking her word for it. Lois grimaced.

Back in the house, Augusta shooed the girls out of the kitchen. They sat in anxious silence in the living room while Augusta cracked the egg in a bowl, then took a store-bought egg from the fridge and cracked it into another bowl. When she was finished, she called the girls back in.

Emma and her sister stood by the counter and stared at the two eggs in front of them. One, with a perfectly round, fat yolk, its yellow center brighter than the sun, swam in a pool of thick, milky goo. The other was small and misshapen, with a dull ginger-orange yolk speckled with tiny brown spots, its gooey pool thin and clear.

Augusta winked at Emma, then turned to Lois. "Can you guess which is which?"

With a little finger, Lois pointed to the plump, yellow one. "Yeah!" she said.

The older woman shook her head. "Actually, it's the little brownish one."

Lois frowned. "But it's worse than the regular kind."

"Worse!" She covered her mouth in shock. "Why would you say it's worse?"

"Because it's small and ugly," Lois said. And Emma's sister was no fool. She was about to be an eight-year-old. *Eight.* A third-grader. So as soon as the words came out, Lois knew what Augusta was getting at. "Oh," she said, nodding.

"That's right. Just because it looks a certain way, doesn't mean it's worse."

"But the taste—"

"Is exceptionally better!" Augusta scooped up the bowls and placed them by the stove. "You'll see."

Lois's egg didn't fry as well as the other one. It was an absolute mess, splattered on the plate, the yolk a fake-tan orange color. But Augusta was right; the taste was exquisite. Like, melt-in-your-mouth exquisite. Smooth and fluffy. In comparison, the one from the fridge came out looking perfect, but it tasted like plastic. *Egg* plastic. It was like *Flowers for Algernon*, except it was eggs for the Jenkins sisters. They could never eat the store-bought kind again.

But before the chicken coop, the farm was, in fact, completely useless.

Tillamook, Oregon was the best of three worlds: mountains, sea, and a huge plot of land to call your own. From this very spot where Emma sat in front of Augusta's house, she could just barely see the open water beyond the empty pasture, the sun rolling off the mountains to her right. Sometimes, during the three years she had lived here, she'd walk outside just to spread out her arms and breathe it all in, filling her lungs with the moist, salty smell of freedom.

Now, on this dreary fall morning, as she sat outside with her coffee, gazing out at the empty farm while waiting for the rain to pour, she could hear the *cluck cluck cluck* of the chickens, the rustling of the hay beneath their tiny feet, the rushed little way they'd waddle up to the top of their coop.

The house was all charm, with big front windows outlined in thick white trim, and flowers that adorned every nook and cranny on the outside, every empty corner and flat surface on the inside. It was so far from everything she'd known before, so close to the sea she could nearly taste the salt on her tongue. She could nearly feel the rolling tide beneath her, as if it would sweep her away, into the ocean.

When she first arrived, Emma's heart had been bitter but hopeful. Then, after a year went by and her mother had died, her heart had hardened again, a heavy stone inside her chest. But stay in Tillamook long enough (and at Augusta's house, no less) and you'll see how your heart will soften again. At least, as much as you'll let it.

It was a culmination of things that had changed Emma in the last two years. The late-night talks with her grandmother. The calm of the farm and the mountains and the sea. The heart in her chest that had slowly begun to heal. It'd had a year of

14

practice already, that expanse of time between the day her father died and the day her mother decided to join him.

The first sign of healing, she knew, was when she started to dance again. It wasn't long after her mother died. Maybe, Emma often thought, her mom's death had even helped. Maybe it had finally clicked, though she wasn't fully conscious of it then, that losing someone you love doesn't stop *you* from existing too. That they don't actually take a part of you with them. Rather, they leave a part of themselves with you.

But her dancing had changed from what it once was. Emma wasn't the Juilliard hopeful anymore, the girl who attended Academy, a private fine arts high school in Manhattan, a school for the elite—and, if not for the elite, it was certainly a school for the rich. Now she was just a broken girl with a too-small leotard and some old worn-out ballet shoes, a girl who had a story to tell. A girl who had all this knotted up pain, and she couldn't hold it in any longer. The story, the pain. Dancing became less a formality, less a means to an end, than it became, for Emma, a release. And unlike the girl she was before, this girl didn't want to share her dancing with others. She wanted it all to herself.

So for two years, Emma danced. In every quiet moment, every minute of time to herself, she danced, making sure no one was around to watch. It wasn't hard to do. Lois was in the sixth grade now (after their first year in Tillamook, Lois was deemed a "gifted student" and encouraged to skip a grade) so she was hardly home during the day. Even after school, Lois kept herself busy. Study groups. Book clubs. (What kind of ten-year-old joins a book club?) She'd even made the volleyball team at her middle school. Lois, like Emma, had inherited the gift of height from their father. Their ambition had come from their mother.

Augusta and her husband, Charles, who she married not long before the girls moved in, took advantage of their surroundings. They went on long hikes, fishing trips, scuba-diving. You have to be outdoorsy, Emma decided, to really live it up in Oregon—to fit in. Augusta and Charles certainly did. They went camping nearly every weekend. And it's not like they were too old to do so. They could handle it, Emma was certain. They were Oregonians.

They invited the girls to join them once. Well, more than once. A *million times* they'd asked them. But Emma and Lois politely declined. It would take a hell of a lot longer than three short years to get these city slickers—longer for Emma, she supposed, than for Lois—to slip on hiking boots and sleep in tents. And besides, knowing Lois would have a full weekend planned already, Emma liked the idea of having the house to herself.

So dancing became her little secret, her private thing, but as she'd started to do it more often, she'd begun to dance more freely. And, though she hoped no one at the farmhouse would find out (performing was an entirely different beast), she'd started to do it less cautiously, too.

Now, as Emma sipped her coffee, swirling its oily texture around her tongue, she looked out at the farm, at the very spot where, she was certain, she'd been caught in the act just the night before.

It had been close to midnight and every light in the house was off. Silence dwelt. Emma was awake in her bed, restless, a feeling of boredom washing over her. She thought of the usual: her father, her mother, her old life in the City. She was twenty years old now, with a busy mind and little to occupy her time. She'd taken a few classes here and there at the local community college, and she worked odd seasonal jobs. Other than that, she just looked after the house and the hens. Cooked and cleaned. Helped Lois with her homework.

(Like the girl even needed it.)

Needless to say, Emma had a lot of time to just sit and think. Think think think. And it was always about the same old stuff.

But on this night, new thoughts began to creep in. She was twenty. *Twenty.* Two-zero. Two whole decades old. And what had she done to show for it? Analyze her childhood half to death? Wallow around in her own self-pity? Pretend she was actually needed on the farm?

These were new kinds of thoughts for her. They didn't make her sad or angry or frustrated. They didn't tug at her heart or make her cry or have her wishing she could join her parents in heaven. For once, she didn't want to curl up into the tiniest ball, tight tight tight, and roll away, out into nothing. No, these new thoughts didn't do that. Instead…they made her *scared*. Who was she? *Who is* Emma Jenkins? And what the hell was she going to do with her life?

Her heart racing with fear, Emma kicked off the sheets and looked around her small bedroom, at the faded curtains and the country furniture, down at the floorboards that were surprisingly quiet. She looked at the mirror in its rusty frame. It had been two years since she started dancing again, as inconspicuously as possible, in this old tiny bedroom. Already, she must have danced a hundred dances here.

The clock on the wall struck twelve, and surely, by now, everyone in the house was asleep. Emma rolled out of bed, her toes cold against the floor, and dressed. Yoga pants. A tank top. Naked feet. She pulled her hair up tight.

She would dance outside this time. The air was heavy and thick, promising rain, and the sky continued to darken, nighttime sinking hard into the farm. She breathed it all in—

18

the smell of the farm, the air, the darkness—as her body slipped into first position. Second. Third. She raised her arms up over her head.

Dancing was like a drug, an addiction. It was like a faucet she couldn't turn off, filling her lungs from within her gut. Once she'd begun, it'd be hours before she could stop. It'd be mere hours afterward that she'd need to do it again. So when a light turned on in the house that night, and a shadowed figure stood in the window, the shadow flitting from window to window, the lights dancing from room to room, she didn't stop. She didn't allow herself to even look.

Emma danced until the sun peeked up at the farm, that moment when the mountains separate darkness from light. Then the clouds had begun to gather, and a steady rain had started to fall. The sky darkened again.

The dancing stopped but Emma's body remained in the pasture, just behind the farmhouse. She sunk to her knees, feeling the mud on her skin where the rain had puddled, and there, dancing turned into something like prayer—directed at no one in particular.

What is my purpose here?

Why haven't you taken me, too?

She waited for several moments. It wasn't a voice that answered her prayer, just the gentle whooshing rush of wind. She lifted her face from her hands, aware of the rain as it slowed around her, then she made her way back to the porch. She curled up on the bench swing and brought two of her fingers to her bottom lip, folding and twisting. Augusta's voice sounded in her head. *That's a terrible habit, girl. Let go of your lips.*

Emma let go. Swaddled in blankets, the rocking of the swing eventually carried her back to sleep.

The rain began to finally spill. Huge, slow drops. As if the sky heard the earth sigh for a song.

Emma set down her coffee and walked to the edge of the porch. She stepped down onto the grassy field. The clouds were colliding, thunder grumbling out of them. The sky opened up again. She tilted her face toward it, allowing the rain to pelt her skin. Then she spread out her arms and smiled.

Show me where I need to be.

Emma stood alone in the pasture, her thoughts burrowing further inward, until, distantly, the sound of a truck jolted her, the gravel vibrating beneath its tires. She knew the sound well by now, having heard it at five o'clock every weekday morning for the last three years, when Charles would leave for work; it was his truck. But what was it doing, starting up now, this late in the morning…on a Thursday?

She picked up her coffee and went back inside. The house remained mysteriously quiet. The coffee pot was still full and steaming, and Lois's backpack sat on the table. *Hadn't she gone to school today?* she thought, fingering the pins and ribbons that adorned it. Beside it, Emma flattened out the newspaper. *Where on Earth did everyone go?*

She reached for the phone and dialed her grandmother's cell.

Augusta answered brightly. "Emma!"

"Augusta, hey," she said. "What's going on? I just heard the truck leave, and Lois's backpack—"

"Oh, dear. I'm so sorry we didn't invite you, but I just thought—"

"Invite me? Where?" Emma could practically *hear* her grandmother smiling through the phone, unbridled by Emma's interruption.

"We've gone camping, sweetheart. Thought you could get an early start, too, so Charles took a couple of days off work. And Lois! Can you believe we got her to finally come with us?"

They'd gone camping…with Lois? And they hadn't told Emma?

And she really started to wonder now, not that she'd have agreed to go, why *didn't* they invite her?

"Oh…" Emma said. She started to pace.

Augusta could hear in her voice, Emma was sure, the questions she knew Emma wouldn't ask out loud. With a mischievous tone, Augusta said, "And anyway...I thought you'd want to start packing."

"Packing? For what?" What game was she playing?

"For your trip." Augusta paused. "You are going, aren't you?"

"Going where, Augusta? What are you trying to tell me?"

"Didn't you get my note?" The cell reception started to fade. "Look on the stove."

Emma turned to face the kitchen, and there it was: a video camera, wrapped in satin, with a ribbon tied around it. Dangling from the ribbon was a set of keys and a note in her grandmother's handwriting. A thousand dollars cash had been tucked into the envelope that lay beside it. Emma set the phone down on the stove, the reception fading in and out. She placed her hands on the satin wrapping, her heart racing as she tore it open.

Her Juilliard audition would be held in the spring, giving her several months to prepare. It was more than she needed. The familiar shiny-yellow keys were attached to a keychain that said *Home*. Emma traced the letters with her finger, her emotions—hope, anxiety, fear—rising up in her chest. The note from her grandmother said: *For your memories, Emma.*

Fleeting thoughts scuttled through her brain like panicked centipedes. She'd fallen in love with dancing again, but what of performing? What of Juilliard? She wasn't that girl anymore…and she hadn't even considered returning home.

The tiny thoughts vanished from the coils in her brain; her mind was empty.

A flight to New York was scheduled to leave at two o'clock the next morning, and Augusta had already booked her a ticket. "Call me when you land," Emma heard her say through the phone.

Then the call dropped.

CHAPTER 2

Emma arrived at Portland International Airport three hours early, the standard earliness for international flights, and though she wasn't traveling out of the country, it certainly felt like it. New York City: a world away.

She made her way to the gate and slipped off her shoes, dozing for a while as she waited for her flight. It had been three years since she was in an airport—and it was *this* airport that was the last she'd been in—and the smell of it was so unique (something like stale coffee mixed with old plastic and freshly-vacuumed carpets), with such heavy emotion attached to it, that she couldn't help but allow it to carry her—gently, swiftly—back to that day. She closed her eyes and drifted there.

They'd had a heck of a time trying to get here. With the images of the attack still fresh in everyone's minds, airports all across the country had barely been functioning, hesitantly so, the people wandering through them all scared-like, stunned and somber, like sad, broken zombies. Direct flights were hard to come by, and wildly expensive, not that it mattered so much to them. Going for frugality anyway, they'd had to stop three times between New York City and Portland, Oregon.

Emma held her sister's hand as they taxied toward their gate. The landings scared Lois, and her face had turned blue.

24

Their mother sat on the other side of Emma, silent and motionless, what would now become something like her permanent state of being.

New security regulations had been put into effect. Changed rules for a changed world. "Post-9/11," their new world was called, and Emma thought it a suitable term, though to be honest, it would be years before it would stop making her cringe. September 11th—the tipping point. The day she'd begun to think of things in terms of *before* and *after*. Couldn't everyone, for once, stop reminding her that she was now in the sad and dark and lonely world of *after*?

Because of the changes, it wasn't Augusta's smiling face they saw when the three of them first got off the plane. Instead it was a slow-moving sea of people, of still expressions, and they seemed to fit right in. Their lostness there.

Emma did her best to swim ahead and navigate through the airport, leading her mother and sister to baggage claim. Augusta, a grandmother the girls had barely known, spotted them first. She didn't say hello or ask how their trip went, just walked right up to them and wrapped them into the circle of her arms, holding them there until their luggage came through on the belt. No one spoke the whole way home.

When they arrived at the farmhouse, Emma's mother and sister headed straight for their beds, exhausted from the journey, the long day, the heaviness of just being there. But

Emma didn't go to bed right away. She stayed downstairs for a while, talking with Augusta. Or more accurately, she stayed downstairs and sat with her grandmother, examining her face as Augusta examined Emma's, each pondering the years that lie ahead. A new journey for both of them.

Finally, after a long while of contemplative gazing, Augusta spoke matter-of-factly. "You won't be staying here forever," she said.

Emma looked at her, *really* looked at her, at the shallow blue of her eyes and the delicate way her blonde hair had grayed. She heard the softness in Augusta's voice, felt her gentle hand over hers. She looked at the smile lines on her grandmother's face.

When Emma's mouth opened to speak, she didn't know what to say. So she closed it tight. Augusta was welcoming her into her home, but only on a temporary basis. Was that it? It seemed she was making her point clear. So what does a person, a seventeen-year-old who's recently been through hell, say to that?

Augusta smiled. "This will be the place Lois remembers twenty years from now, when she thinks of home. I'll do my best to help your mother teach her and raise her up right. She'll have happy memories here."

"And my mother?"

"I love my daughter. I love her to the end of my being, the same way she loves you. You do know how much she loves you, don't you?"

Emma mouthed a little *yes* and nodded, but did she really believe it? Since her father died, her mother hadn't acted so loving toward her—or her sister. She hadn't acted so…anything. Just this still, broken, empty shell of a woman. It wasn't even her idea to bring them here. It was Augusta's.

Augusta went on. "Oh, I can't be certain of your mother's future. That's up to her. Whether she'll decide to stay here or go off on her own and carve out something new, I don't know."

"You think she'll leave us?"

Augusta's hand grew firm over Emma's. "Please, Emma, don't misunderstand me. I'm not saying anything, one way or another. My point is that it's uncertain. Your mother and I…we hadn't left things between us on the best of terms."

"What happened?" The question flew from Emma's mouth.

"Maybe another time. My point is that I have no certainties regarding your mother, but I'm certain for Lois. She'll grow up here. She'll be happy. She'll stay in my care, and I'll raise her up right. I promise you that."

Emma thought of her mother. "You're promising *me*?"

"Yes, Emma." Augusta smiled. "I'm promising *you*."

Me, Emma thought. As if she was responsible for Lois now. She let that sink in for a while, until the words that had started their whole conversation jolted her back to here, on the couch, sitting across from her grandmother. *Her mean, cold grandmother.* "You had said—"

"Right." Augusta sat up straighter, pulled her hand away from Emma's. "I want you to know that I won't have you staying here longer than absolutely necessary."

"Necessary for what?"

"For you to move on!" She nearly laughed. "I've seen your grades, Emma. I've seen your dancing, too. That routine you've been practicing for your Juilliard audition? Your mother sent me the tapes."

"What are you saying, Grandmother?"

"I'm saying you have a bigger future than what this useless little farm can offer. You have strength and ambition and talent, Emma. Do you hear me? You have dreams, I know you do, and you have all the means in the world to reach them. You know you still have the means, don't you? You know what your father left you, right?" She didn't give Emma time to answer. "And when you're ready—and you'll be ready, someday—I'll see to it that you go and you follow those dreams."

Emma found herself nodding, hearing the truth in her

grandmother's words but wondering if she had those dreams anymore. Or if maybe her dreams had already changed, morphed into something more impossible, something that wouldn't take money or hard work or talent to achieve. Because really, all she wanted then was her old life again. Their home. The City. Dad.

She didn't notice her grandmother get up until the imprint she'd left on the couch had started to rise up again, air pushing through waves of fabric. She heard the older woman's voice from the stairway. "And one more thing," her grandmother said. "Please, call me Augusta. 'Grandmother' makes me feel old. And I'm only fifty-seven."

"OK," Emma said. "Goodnight, Augusta."

"Goodnight, dear."

Now, as she sat up in the stiff, faux-leather chair, her eyes fluttering open, a warmth rose up from her feet, through her legs, her arms, filling her chest. Augusta knew. She knew *Emma*. And in spite of everything, all that had happened in the last three years, Augusta never gave up on her. She never gave up on Emma's dreams. Even if Emma did for a while.

She looked around again at the still, quiet airport, then up at the clock in front of her. She had more than an hour before her flight would leave. The plane hadn't even arrived yet. She pulled her carry-on up to her lap and dug around for something to pass the time. An iPod. A book. But she came up empty. Why hadn't she thought to bring those things?

Then, when she reached in deeper, Emma felt the satin as it brushed her fingers, remembering now that she'd packed the camera in her carry-on.

It struck her that there are moments in life when it seems like your mind is a separate entity from your being, and smarter than you are. It didn't make sense to her then—and it doesn't now, really—because our mind is practically *who* we are, the sum of our memories, the thing with which we interpret the world around us. But in that moment, Emma knew her mind had been thinking...even if she wasn't.

Her mind knew not to pack a book or an iPod. It knew to swaddle the camera with blankets and tie the satin around it, then shove it to the bottom of her carry-on. It knew to arrive here at least an hour earlier than she needed to.

Emma sat up straighter, sliding her butt as far back in the seat as she could. She unwrapped the camera and crossed her legs beneath her, then tilted the lens to her face and flipped on the camera's switch. Her breaths were steady, in and out, as she willed her heart to slow. She hesitated, just for a moment, wondering what she would say, and keenly aware she was in a public place, even if the public technically wasn't.

Where was everyone?

And then, with a steadier voice than she had expected, Emma started to speak, her thoughts unfolding naturally as they came.

It's early Friday morning here in Portland, Oregon. My name is Emma Jenkins, and this is day one of my journey. We'll call it My Remembering Journey. *Sounds silly, I know, but Augusta thinks it will help me remember. And more than anything, I want to remember. Because I was there, I know I was, and I hate that I've forgotten. The last time he smiled at me, told me he loved me. His final breath. I have a right to those memories and I want them back.*

Augusta says I can catalogue all of my memories here, no matter how old or new they are, and once the wheels start turning, she says, maybe the forgotten memories will surface. I'm not sure I believe her yet, but I'll try anything.

Anything to help me remember that day.

The thing of it is, I think I have too many memories. I don't know where to begin. So I'll start with what I don't remember, and that's the day my father died.

You've probably never met Henry Jenkins, my dad, but unlike me, I'm sure you can remember where you were when he died. You can remember who you were with, why you were there, what you were talking about. You remember it vividly, as if it were yesterday: the awful sights, the piercing sounds, the vile stench that would drape the City for days, weeks. You remember…because everyone *remembers*.

Except me. I don't remember where I was when my father died, or what I was doing, or how it felt when I first found out. Did I think about all of the others who had died? Did I think about what it all meant? I don't remember who it was who delivered the news to me, or how I might've reacted to hearing it.

Because, you see, I have been blessed with the ability to forget. Or so I'm told.

But I do remember the days and weeks that followed. I remember how the fine ash and dust lingered in the air, how everything turned up in piles. Piles of paper, of people. I remember how the streets went quiet, how the entire City became sad and somber and wounded, reeling from its open sore. And I remember the handbills, so many handbills that flew up, littering the City as they hung. So many hopeful faces of those who were missing. Hopeful, desperate faces.

They've been coming back to me lately—the memories, everything from that day. They come in waves, in dreams. For a while, it was all anyone talked about, especially in the City. I gathered bits and pieces from what I'd heard—the planes, the towers, the billowing smoke. The hate that caused it all. I'd seen it on video, even, because who hasn't watched the videos or seen the pictures and just been sucked in, unable to tear their eyes away from it? And I can't ever tear my eyes away from it, because I know he *was* there.

32

I may not remember that day for myself, but I remember my father well. He was a quiet man, strong and patient. He doted on me, my mother and sister. He was handsome, loving, forgiving. I couldn't believe some of the things he forgave us for. But it's funny, after my sister and I—and even my mother, sometimes—had done what we thought was the absolute worst thing we had ever done, and Daddy still forgave us, it didn't make us think we could do whatever we wanted. It didn't make us think we could run the show, like, Hey, it's OK, Daddy will forgive us for this.

Instead, it made us want to always please him, to live our lives out just to please him, so he'd never have to forgive us again.

By now, the seats began to fill. Emma's emotions were rising up again, hot and thick. She looked around the gate area and managed to swallow the sobs that had started to lump in the back of her throat. Had anyone heard her speaking? Did anyone notice her face flush red, that she was on the verge of crying? There were businessmen and women carrying briefcases; teenagers with headphones plugged in their ears; flight attendants strolling by with their wheeled luggage. An elderly woman sat across from her, crocheting. When no one seemed to look her way, Emma breathed a sigh of relief.

She sat still, cradling the camera with open hands, focusing on the flashing light that reminded her she hadn't turned it off.

She tried to think of her father again, of anything else she might have to say. Then, slowly, the sadness started to fade, replaced by something warmer, stronger. The lump in her throat sank to her chest. Emma wasn't thinking of her father anymore, but of her mother. When she began to speak again, her voice was soft and broken.

My mom wasn't so forgiving. I'd even heard her say once that she didn't forgive my father. The entire year after Dad's death, she seemed to keep these grudges inside of her, locked up tight. How could he just go and die like that, she said. How could she survive without him?

But to everyone else in the City, my father was a hero. I was reminded everywhere I went. And I mean everywhere. *Don't get me wrong, I loved my father, but do you have any idea how it feels to be constantly reminded of something you can't even fully remember yourself? Especially when that something still stings? As if I had cuts and scrapes and bruises all over my body (even* inside*) and everyone could see them. And everyone wanted to ask me about them.*

That's not why I ended up leaving the City, though it would have been reason enough. To just get away, to start over in a place where no one knew my story, a place where it'd be OK that I'd forgotten, because maybe they'd all forgotten by then, too. As it turned out, my sister and I didn't have a choice in the matter. Our mother was barely surviving and the two of us weren't old enough, or ready enough, to brave the City on our own. So we sought refuge, or rather, we were rescued—by our mother's mother, Augusta. She'd just remarried, had a little farmhouse in Oregon, had a heart too big not to take us in.

So that would be that, I thought. I'd attend community college in Oregon, learn just enough to get by. I'd make new friends, or not. I'd lie in the sun on the shore. I'd start over, because no one there would know my story. Because my story was just beginning.

CHAPTER 3

The early mornings in New York City had been consistently damp and cool. Emma arrived a little past nine with only one suitcase aside from her carry-on, which she'd stuffed with makeup and hairspray, a leotard, warm-ups, and the same old ballet shoes she'd had since high school, shoes that had gone unworn for far too long.

Frank, her driver, stood in the open doorway. He called to her from across the foyer. "Will you be all right here, Miss Jenkins?"

Emma turned to look at him, smiling courteously. "Yes, sir," she said. "Thank you very much." She watched as he set her luggage on the hardwood floor of the entryway, then he nodded, tipped his hat and left, closing the door gently behind him. A heavy sigh escaped her lips.

The furniture was draped with sheets, but even after three years her family's belongings stood untouched in their place. Their winter coats still hung in the closets; picture frames collected dust on the dressers and mantels; an old teddy bear sat between the pillows on her bed. Though her memory hadn't fully come back to her yet, she could tell her home had remained unchanged, as if the powers of war and loss and fear hadn't been strong enough to penetrate this place.

Emma returned to the front door and reached for her

luggage, then made her way to the bedroom upstairs. She plopped her luggage on top of the bed and walked around her childhood room, staring, first, at the pictures and trophies on the dresser. The trio of gold-dipped ballerinas; the plaque from her first recital at Academy; a picture of the little red-haired, freckle-faced girl she had once been, smiling wide, donning her first tutu. It was green and pink and awfully gaudy. Staring at the photo, a hint of a smile appeared on her face.

Through the open windows, bright beams of mid-morning light seeped in, flitting across the forgotten items. Dust particles hung still in the sun's rays. Emma took a deep breath and made her way to the center of the room where she sank to her knees on the floor. She looked up, her eyes scanning the room, taking it all in while a flood of memories came rushing back. Her family, her childhood. She swam through the memories of elementary school and middle school, through early recitals and young friendships, family vacations and childhood pets. And then, with the force of a tsunami, high school hit her right in the face.

She remembered being *that girl* in high school. You know the one. That girl everyone thinks is strange because she keeps to herself and takes her studies seriously. But she didn't care. She'd even convinced herself she was *that girl* who everyone pretends to avoid but secretly wishes they could be friends with. The more she thought about it, even long after she left

Academy, the more she believed she was probably right about that.

Not that Emma was a total bitch in high school, though the label had been thrown her way more than once. She was nice to those who were nice to her, and even to those who weren't always. She was driven and serious, even beyond the standards at Academy. She was quiet, too. A total introvert. And she had no idea how to handle relationships—friendships and otherwise. Emma was just…misunderstood. Or maybe she was completely understood, but isn't it harder to believe that those who know you well are the ones who hate you the most?

The real reason she was so hated, Emma reconciled, is that physically she was the peak of perfection in high school. Wafer-thin with a flawless peaches-and-cream complexion, big emerald green eyes flecked with gold in the center, and long, thick auburn hair. Plus she was smart, and she had real talent too. And at Academy, talent mattered. Talent was everything. So *what* if her only real friend was Chloe Adams, an equally serious girl who had little more time for Emma than Emma had for her? She would dance her way into Juilliard, and for a time, nothing could get in the way of that.

Emma enrolled at Academy with a double major in modern dance and ballet, but she dabbled around with the piano and creative writing, among other things. She was obsessive and motivated, qualities that emanated brightest when they came from her art.

Once, in the ninth grade, Emma wrote a short story about a girl named Rose who went to the beach to collect seashells. In the story, Rose spends the entire day there, picking up only the best ones, and she's able to find everything she's looking for. Smooth shells, pink shells. Shells with holes in them to hang on necklaces. Afterward, she brings them home to her family and they all sit around the fire examining them, praising the girl for a job well done. It was ten thousand words about a pretty girl and her pretty seashells.

When Emma turned the story in to her lit professor at Academy, the teacher frowned. "This is no good," she said. She'd never been one to sugarcoat things.

It really stung. Emma was a mere freshman, still unable to handle such brute rejection, and so she hadn't understood her professor's response. The details were intricate, were they not? The writing was beautiful. It was the highest quality prose the woman had ever held in her hands! How could she not have recognized that? Emma thought she must have been a hack or something. It was the only explanation.

"There's no tension, Emma," she said. "Where's the conflict?"

"There isn't any," Emma told her. "It's a happy story about a girl and some seashells." Keyword: *happy*.

"No, no, no." Frown lines played around the old woman's lips. She shook her head. "A happy story is not one without conflict. Weren't you paying attention in class?"

Yeah, Emma thought. *She's a hack all right.*

So Emma went home and rewrote the story. In the second draft, Rose gets lost collecting her seashells. Her family waits for her by the pier, but she wanders far out. Clouds darken overhead and roll in quickly. Mist blankets the shore. She can no longer see the pier. When she looks out at the ocean, she sees the waves build in intensity and rush up to her feet. She hurries to gather the seashells, but as quickly as she touches them they break apart into tiny fragments of sand that sift between her fingers and fly away, into the sea. She runs after the sand, as futile as chasing the wind, until she's chest-deep in the water. The waves continue to build and crash around her. Soon, Rose loses her bearings and the storm swallows her up, burying her body beneath the weight of the ocean and the beautiful seashells she'd been working so hard to collect.

Emma slammed the story down on her teacher's desk. *How's that for conflict, you bitter old crone?*

Come to think of it, maybe Emma *was* a bitch.

As she sat on the floor in the middle of her bedroom,

Emma actually laughed out loud at her former self. At the insecurities she'd worked so hard to cover up; her old childish stubbornness, selfishness, and narrow-minded thinking; at the feelings—not just hers, but the feelings of others—that she had ignored.

She was laughing, quite frankly, because at this point in her journey home, she still wasn't allowed to cry.

Looking around, Emma remembered how lively her room used to be, how free it had once made her feel. It was her sanctuary, the place she'd go to get lost, to dream and dance, no matter how frustrating life could be, no matter what was happening in the world outside. Now, the room was still, devoid of energy and life, thickly coated in dust. There was nothing left of it, it seemed. Nothing but the deep, howling echo of her childhood.

Emma stood. She hadn't returned to the City to sit alone, pining in her bedroom. She had come back to dance, and also, she had come back to remember. But what, specifically? Anything, she guessed. Whatever came to mind.

It didn't matter if her first thoughts were seemingly random and insignificant. The important ones would come.

My parents thought I might have been a lesbian, and in a strange way, I almost thought it could have been true.

I overheard them one night, early in the spring of 2001, talking in hushed whispers at the dining room table, steam rising in puffs from the coffee in front of them. I sat near the stairs on the second floor of our home, hidden behind the mahogany railing. My hair, what had been long and thick just the day before, was cut short, revealing my face. Its delicate features. Thin lips, bright green eyes, a turned-up nose. I felt completely exposed.

As I sat and listened, I fingered the longest tendrils of my new pixie cut, the pieces that swept across my brows. I smiled as I thought of shampooing and brushing and tying it up in a tight bun on top of my head. All the things that would no longer consume me.

My Freedom Cut, *I'd called it.*

"I blame myself," Mom said, staring into her cup of coffee. "We chase away every boy she brings home, telling her to focus. Juilliard, Juilliard, Juilliard.*" She paused to gaze at my dad. "Not that there have been many boys around lately."*

Dad nodded. "It's her dream though, isn't it? Dancing, Juilliard. We keep telling her to focus, but I don't think she needs us to. I think she tells herself often enough, don't you?"

"Yes, you're right." She managed a smile. "But then she goes and chops off her hair, and I just have to wonder—"

"Frances, your head is in overdrive." He set down his coffee and reached for her hand. "You're overthinking this. Emma is seventeen. She's just starting to find her way. She's just learning who she is."

42

"Well, while she's off learning who she is, I feel like I don't know a thing about her anymore."

Silence fell over them for several moments, until my dad turned to my mom and said, "Maybe our daughter is a lesbian." I inched closer against the railing, as if to prepare for confirmation.

Mom's mouth fell open. "Henry!"

With a patient smile, he held a finger to her lips. "Well, you said it yourself, didn't you? She hasn't brought any boys around, and she's got a short haircut now. Evidence clearly suggests…"

A smile made its way to her lips.

"All I'm saying is, if there's something important that Emma needs to tell us, she'll tell us. She always does."

"Does she?" Mom asked.

I inched away from the railing and made my way to my bedroom. As I lay awake in bed that night, I thought about what they'd said. I was pretty sure I wasn't a lesbian, and my father was right—I knew I could talk to them about important things. As long as they were really important. I knew not to bother them otherwise.

I tried to convince myself that I wasn't a lesbian. I never thought about girls as anything other than friends, and I wouldn't have had any more time for a girlfriend than I had for a boyfriend. And to think I was making some sort of statement with my new haircut? That was ridiculous. It was my Freedom Cut, not my Coming-Out-of-the-Closet Cut. Sometimes my mother had the wildest imagination.

Nonetheless, I mulled it over all night. Like I wasn't quite sure either way. By the end of the following day, though, I was fully convinced I was straight.

The phone rang from the kitchen downstairs. It sounded faint—she'd hardly noticed it at first—but when it finally registered, she ran downstairs and peeked at the Caller ID: Chloe Adams, fellow Academian and former dancer-friend. Her *best friend*, Emma thought, second only to Henry Hayes. She had told Chloe she'd be returning to the City, but hadn't actually expected her call.

"Hey, Chlo."

"Emma! Long time no talk. How are you settling in?" Chloe's voice was friendly and cheerful.

"OK. I haven't been here long. Frank just dropped me off a little while ago."

"Oh, Frank! How is he?"

Emma took a seat at the counter, her brows furrowed in confusion. *Why is she acting so bubbly?* If it was just for sympathy, Emma would prefer it if she hadn't called. She lowered her tone and answered shortly. "He's OK, Chlo. What did you—"

"Good, good. Well I just wanted to call and check on you. Make sure you're all right."

"Why wouldn't I be all right?"

"No specific reason. You need help with anything? Grocery shopping? Unpacking?"

"No, I'm fine. Really."

"Oh, Emma, I don't mean to get in your space. I'm sure you need a little time to yourself. Get settled in and all."

"Right, yeah," Emma said, more curtly than she had intended. "Sorry, I didn't mean—"

"No, no. That's OK." Chloe paused. "Hey, Em?"

"Yeah?"

"Have you talked with Henry yet?"

It was the first time in a long time that Emma heard his name spoken out loud (of course, when it wasn't in reference to her father). Henry Hayes, just a single, simple name. It had lost all meaning in the last three years. So why had her cheeks warmed, her breath hitched, her heart started beating like a drum in her chest?

"Why would I have talked to him?" she finally managed. "Didn't he move back to Albuquerque, like, three years ago?" And what did Chloe care, anyway? She had never been friends with Henry. Not like Emma had been.

"Oh, right," Chloe said. "Well, I was just curious."

"OK…"

"If you need anything, you know where to find me."

"Thanks, Chloe."

"Yeah, anytime." Chloe paused before adding, "I've missed

you."

The drumming in Emma's chest silenced. First the phone call, then the cheerfulness, the inquisitiveness, and now...*I've missed you?* Who was this Chloe Adams imposter?

Emma glanced suspiciously at the phone and said, simply, "Me too, Chloe."

I just spoke with my old friend, Chloe. She was acting strange, but I won't dwell on it. People haven't known how to act around me since Dad died.

I'm remembering a lot right now. Stuff about high school, mostly. But also, stuff about Henry.

We were opposites in so many ways. Though I was five-foot-six, at nearly six feet tall he towered over me. He had light, shaggy brown hair and dark brown eyes—not piercing brown or boring brown, but soft, chocolate brown that melted when he glanced over at me and smiled. Which was always, because Henry was just that way. Always happy, always smiling. It didn't matter what other people might have thought of him. Henry was who he was, and he wouldn't have changed for the world.

And in that way, Henry and I were quite the same.

Henry didn't fit in at Academy. He wasn't polished or very well educated. His mother had stumbled upon more money than they'd ever dreamed of when she started a business selling other people's stuff on the

Internet. They moved from Albuquerque, New Mexico and bought a big loft on the Upper West Side, paid cash to Academy for the final year and a half of Henry's high school tuition. They weren't new money or old money; they were lucky money, *lucky money that could only afford less than two full years of proper schooling for Henry. Needless to say, the family wasn't highly respected in their new community of 'peers.'*

*That's what I liked about him though. Henry was edgy, grungy, a rebel. He was so…*non-routine.

Henry's attendance at Academy certainly rocked the school. The first time I saw him was in a music theory class we shared together. It was the day after I'd lied awake all night, mulling over the talk my parents had about me being a lesbian. I was sitting up perfectly straight in front of a piano, my short hair pinned back from my face, my lips pursed like I was really something serious, playing Pachelbel's Canon in D. *Henry walked in from the other side of the room. This skinny, scruffy thing with dirty shoes, an old Pink Floyd T-shirt and a vintage-looking acoustic guitar strung across his chest. I just about lost it. My jaw dropped open and my fingers stumbled over the keys. The room silenced.*

Ten minutes or so later, the class had all taken their seats for the lesson to begin: Scales and Modes. Henry let out an enormous sigh from the rear of the classroom. Twenty sets of eyes glared back at him. At the very least, he did seem slightly embarrassed by the outburst. Just slightly.

"Focus," Professor Heisel demanded. All eyes whipped back to the front of the room, but I couldn't pay attention. I looked at Henry, just two rows up, with his head down, unruly strands of hair covering his eyes, his

lips mouthing a song as he strummed his guitar. He paid no attention to what was happening with the lesson, and neither could I.

My eyes remained fixed on him, and it was like the volume of the entire room had been turned down in my brain, and all I could hear was the strumming of his guitar. All I could do was watch as he played.

Later that morning, right before lunch, I had ballet. I remember, because I remember thinking it was perfect—how I never liked to dance on a full stomach. There were five other girls in the class, including Chloe, and it went exactly how you might imagine a ballet class at Academy would go. Quiet and serious. Focused. It was the advanced class, but even for us the combination was difficult. And the professor, Charlotte Briganly—who we called "Birdlady" because of her tiny pointed nose, her colorful attire, and the ear-splitting way she'd squawk orders at us— didn't exactly make things easier.

I had an advantage in ballet, being tall and slender, able to control my body with natural ease. Plus it was my main focus, the thing I cared about perfecting most. And so, as the other girls grew more and more frustrated, Chloe included, I nailed the combo, executed it with flawless, fluid movements.

From the back of the room, I could still hear Birdlady squawk. "Emma Jenkins! Darling! Will you come up here please?"

Skill hadn't yielded confidence yet. Not for me. So with my head low, my shoulders hunched ungracefully, I tip-toed up to the front of the room. "Yes, ma'am?"

"That was fantastic! Please, dear, show these ladies the combination."
With her hands on my shoulders, she turned me around to face the group.
I remember, quite distinctly, how my blood burned beneath my cheeks. I
stepped into first position as she shouted, "Five, six, seven, eight!*"*

Afterward, I lifted my head to face the girls. I could see the frustration
on their faces, the eye-rolling, the snickering, but it was Chloe's face I
noticed the most. Her eyes landed right on mine, filled with
disappointment. I hadn't meant to do that, *I wanted to say.* I hadn't
meant to be such a show-off, but don't you see? Birdlady *made*
me. *I watched as Chloe shook her head, so slow it was hardly noticeable.*

When the bell rang, I was so relieved to escape the tension. I quickly
gathered my things, then nudged Chloe and motioned her aside.

"Lunch?" I asked.

"Not today," she said. "I think I'll stick around here and practice.
I'm not too hungry anyway." She was barely looking at me.

I said nothing else, just nodded in understanding and walked away.

I'd been an emotional wreck all day, and now I wanted more than
*anything to punch something, or some*one. *My parents for thinking I was*
a lesbian (clearly, they didn't know about Henry Hayes yet); Birdlady for
calling me out like that; Chloe for holding it against me. Had I even
actually *done anything wrong in there?*

I stormed out of the room, not knowing that Henry was standing just
outside. I crashed into him, and with the jolt I felt the tears that had been
pooling in my eyes begin to spill down my cheeks. Shocked to see him, and
embarrassed to be crying, I sucked in my breath and wiped the tears from

my face.

"Hey," he said.

"Hello," I said brusquely before turning my face away.

Before I could leave, he stuck his arm straight out. "Hey, I'm—"

"I know who you are. You're the new kid. Harry, is it?" Right, like I didn't know his name. He was more than memorable; plus my father's *name was Henry.*

"Actually, it's Henry." He shrugged, as if it didn't matter that I'd gotten his name wrong, and his hand was still held out toward me, bobbing up and down as he tried to keep up with my pace. I kept my eyes forward as we walked.

After several moments, Henry finally retracted his arm, tucking his hand in his pocket. Then he said something that surprised me, and I could feel my cheeks grow hot as they reddened. "So I see you're a fan of the guitar."

I stopped where I was in the middle of the hallway and turned to face him. "What?"

"I saw you in class today. You were watching me play."

"I was not.*"*

"Sure you were," Henry said, smiling cheekily.

I shook my head and continued to walk. "If you saw me watching you, it's only because of how ridiculous you look. We have a dress code here, in case you haven't noticed."

Henry looked down at his dirty sneakers and tattered jeans. "Yeah,

I've noticed." He shrugged, and I couldn't help but smile. Then there was a long, awkward moment of silence, and I spent it gazing at Henry. He was handsome, especially for a high school boy. Full lips, high cheekbones, a strong jaw. His eyes were almond-shaped, set deeply, and his hair was long and messy, matted strands sweeping across his brows. He grinned, and his whole face lit up, his eyes crinkling, a shallow dimple poking into his cheek. I have to be careful with this one, I thought. Fucking dimples.

"You haven't told me your name yet," he said, interrupting my thoughts.

"It's Emma." I reached out my hand and placed it in his. "Emma Jenkins."

"Nice to meet you, Emma, Emma Jenkins. Can I walk you to the dining hall?"

I hesitated before saying, "Henry, I have to be honest with you. I'm really not here for a boyfriend. I'm here to dance, OK? I'm here to learn, and if that makes me weird or crazy or strange, well, I don't really care. But…I just…I can't be distrac—"

I paused as a smile spread wide across Henry's face. He inched closer to me. "Relax," he said. "I'm not asking you out. But I could really use some help getting adjusted here. I mean, look at me." He gestured to his attire again. "I look like I stumbled in here off the street."

I was so presumptuous! The smile from earlier dripped down my throat and into my stomach, and I laughed. Nervous laughter. Gut-wrenching laughter. It spread to Henry too, and we were both bent over at *the waist, choking with laughter. It was the most ridiculous sight, us laughing our asses off in the middle of the hallway at the most dignified high school in Manhattan. But Henry didn't care, and so neither did I.*

"So, lunch?" he asked. He put his hands together in front of him, and his puppy eyes grew big and pleading.

"OK," I relented. "I'll let you walk me to lunch. I'm starving, anyway."

Henry smiled brightly and brushed his hair away from his face, revealing those big chocolate-almond eyes again. "Great. And I assume you know where the dining hall is?"

"Follow me."

We sat down with our lunches, facing each other across the table, and Henry went straight for the kill. "So tell me, Emma. How much do you really like all of this?"

"All of what?"

"This…life. Dancing, performing, honing for Juilliard. You know, this…Academy life."

I said the first thing that came to mind. "I love it."

"Really?"

"Yeah, Henry. It's the most important thing to me."

He took a deep breath, as if to consider. "Heavy," he said.

"What do you mean?"

He hesitated, but just briefly. "Emma—and I mean this in the nicest way, believe me—it's just that, well, you don't really seem to fit in here.

52

At Academy, I mean."

I didn't know whether to feel angry or to be shocked at how he'd guessed so quickly. I did fit in, in the obvious ways, but anyone could tell you that I didn't, either.

"How could you say that? I'm one of the top dancers here. I earn excellent grades, and—"

He was shaking his head as I spoke. "I'm not talking about your talent."

"What more do you need here than that?" I asked, smiling grimly.

He looked at me, his eyes narrowed. "It's interesting to note," he said, changing the subject, "a lot of Juilliard students aren't actually rich. They get scholarships. From what I hear, the school is very generous."

"Who says I'm rich?"

Henry huffed. "Oh, you're definitely rich."

"Why would you say that?"

"Because you don't care what anyone thinks of you."

"Neither do you," I said.

"No, but for different reasons."

I sat back and glared at him. "You never answered my question."

Henry leaned in and said, "Passion, Emma. You need passion."

"Are you saying I don't have—"

"No, no, no. I'm saying—and I know I'm presuming audaciously here, what with it being my first day and all—but what I'm saying is…it seems like you're the only one here who does."

I looked away and let those words sit between us for a long while before turning back to him. "So what about you, Henry? I assume you don't care about fitting in, considering who you've chosen as your first friend."

He nodded. "I know there's no way I could fit in here. You see, Emma, I have way too much passion."

I wasn't sure what he meant by that, but I let it be. He'd go on if he wanted to, that much I knew already, and so we sat together in the silence and ate. When we were finished and the bell sounded to tell us lunch was over, Henry faced me with a smile. "So, we're friends?" he asked.

And I said, "Yeah, Henry. We're friends."

CHAPTER 4

They say you can't go home again, but who would want to? It will never be the same as it was before you left, because *you* won't be the same. You'll have changed, that much is certain, and the contrast will be striking—breathtaking—once you set foot in that place. It will have worsened, most likely, the new sight of it leaving you with that longing, sick feeling in your stomach, telling you that you'll never get it back again, that those days are really over.

Or worse, it will have improved, become something far better than you remember it being, now that you've left it alone. Because maybe home is better off without you, after all.

Emma didn't have a good reason not to come back sooner. Come to think of it, she didn't have a good reason to leave in the first place. Sure, she had reasons, but she couldn't honestly say that any of them were *good*.

It's not like she was some kid when she left, like she couldn't have handled life on her own. She was closer to being an adult than a child. And she was just months away from graduating Academy, months that would have led to a Juilliard acceptance, months she could have spent living with Chloe. Or on her own. But she chose the easier route: she chose to run away. And worse, she called it a "rescue," as if Augusta had saved her from a life in the City that hadn't really been worth living.

Four years of Academy tuition, right down the drain. It was the least of Emma's concerns.

She couldn't say, either, that she never had a longing to return, a little voice in her head that said *go*. Her family's home was still in their name. And Juilliard wasn't going anywhere. She was certain Henry had left, and she and Chloe weren't that close, as far as friends go. So when the little voice showed up and started taunting her, again and again, *go go go*, you know what Emma said? She said, *Why?* Or more specifically, *Why now?* She said she'd go back eventually, when she was ready, like Augusta told her she would. But that wasn't true. Emma wasn't waiting; she was *afraid*.

She hadn't known yet that you can fool your friends, and you can fool your family, and you can even fool yourself, but you can't fool the little voice inside your head.

Emma sat on the middle of the bed and tucked her feet into the blankets. She was holding the camera with its lens toward her and the light flashing, and all of a sudden, her whole body started to tremble. She was afraid that everything had changed since she left. Academy, Juilliard, her friends. They'd all moved on without her. The entire City was fine without her, and was she surprised? She was just one person in a sea of millions. *Tens* of millions. So why did she even come back?

Then Emma realized, all of this time, that hadn't been what she was so afraid of. She was more afraid that nothing back home had changed at all.

When her eyes began to water, Emma flipped off the camera and looked around her room, catching her breath, then she wiped her face with her hands. The days in Tillamook had gone by quietly, serenely, and it had been a while since she'd done so much talking. But her little diatribe didn't leave her feeling relieved. Instead it left her feeling empty and dry, like her mouth was stuffed with cotton, like her insides had been wrung.

Emma knew well by then what depression felt like. That numbing feeling that starts in your belly and spreads itself outward, to your arms and your legs, a swelling that reaches up to your face, your mind, until your entire self begins to shut down. And you don't know that you can ever shake it. You don't know if you even want to.

That's how it felt when she turned off the camera.

Yeah, Henry, she'd said. *We're friends.*

Not anymore, they weren't.

And Chloe's words: *Have you talked to Henry yet?* Why would Chloe think she had?

Emma fought hard against the sadness. It had been like a tide all day, creeping up before easing back down, higher and higher each time, an erosion that was almost physically noticeable. If the tide were depression, though, it was Emma who controlled the moon.

She went downstairs for a glass of water and brought it back up to her room, where Yo-Yo Ma's *Solo* album from 1999 was still in the CD player on her dresser. It was exactly what Emma needed the day she left home, and it was exactly what she needed today as well. She pressed play and stood for several moments, allowing the *Appalachia Waltz* to swim up through her bloodstream and spread to her limbs before pooling in the core of her heart. She felt cradled in its peace.

As the music played, she made her rounds throughout the house. She tore the sheets from the furniture and blew dust from the frames and the miscellaneous items that splattered across the tables, dressers, and countertops. She spread the curtains wide and lifted the windows open, sunlight beaming into the house. When she was finished, she went to the kitchen and set a pot of coffee to brew. Then it was time to turn up the music. There would be no more pining, no more feeling sorry for herself. It was time to carry on, to move forward, to live life again.

With the music blaring, coffee in hand, Emma made her way to the center of her bedroom. She rolled up the Oriental rug and set it against the wall, and then, after several deep, shaky breaths, she set down her coffee and began to dance. Slowly at first, managing to find her rhythm again. It was the real reason she had returned from Augusta's house in Tillamook. Emma was ready to dance again. She was ready to audition for Juilliard.

And in that moment, as the room spun around her and she gave herself fully up to the dance, Emma knew she was more than ready. She knew, now, that nothing would stop her from reaching her dreams. Not the memories that she'd lost, not the sadness that would creep.

It wasn't the first time dancing had overtaken her like that.

It was a Thursday, early in August of 2001, when the fall semester had just started up again. Henry and Emma were sitting together in their late afternoon music class. He was goofing around, trying to make her laugh. It was an impossible endeavor, and he'd tried everything: reaching over the table in front of her to draw cartoons or write silly little phrases on her notepad; impersonating the professor every time he turned around; playing the air-cello like he had any idea what he was doing. All the while Emma remained composed, sitting up tall and stoic, her eyes opened wide to keep from losing focus. There was no way Henry would see her break.

When it was over, the students flooded out of the classroom. Even Professor Heisel refused to stick around, sauntering off to the café for his daily PB&J sandwich and blueberry yogurt. Henry would leave with the group, saying his farewells with the usual fist-bump and left-eye-wink, and Emma would stay behind and practice. It was easier to concentrate in the quiet.

But this time, Henry stayed.

"Aren't you going?" she asked.

"Nah," he said. "I thought I'd stay back a while, see what it is you do here after class. It's a little weird, I hope you know. You being in here by yourself."

"Yeah, I know." Emma gathered her notes and her bag and stood up from the seat, then made her way down to what they dotingly referred to as "the pulpit" because Mr. Heisel had the air of a pastor. He didn't teach them music and composition; he preached it.

Henry followed closely behind her. "So what's on the menu today?" he asked. "Piano, clarinet, maybe some bass guitar?" He was kidding about the bass guitar.

"Dance, actually."

He shot Emma a puzzled look. "But there's a studio for that."

"I know." She was wearing a leotard beneath her dress, and like nothing, she slipped out of the dress and let it drop to the floor, a puddle of daisies at her feet. Henry's eyes grew wide at first, his face flushed with color, but he didn't turn away. Emma knelt down and gathered up the fabric of the dress, then reached inside the bag for her ballet shoes.

She sat down, her butt flat on the hardwood floor, and began to wrap her feet. Then she continued. "The studio is where I go to learn, and learning is frustrating. I can't let go there. I can't dance for *me*." Henry's gaze softened. "It's just bad *feng shui*," she said smartly. She knew Henry thought things like *feng shui* were a load of crap. It was right up there with organic foods and yoga and aromatherapy.

"Who knew you were such a hippie."

She rolled her eyes and tightened the last bit of ribbon around her ankle. "So why are you here, anyway?"

Henry took a deep breath and stepped closer to Emma. He reached for her hands and his eyes melted into hers. *Oh my god, he's actually going to do it. He's going to kiss me.* Emma reminded herself not to let him. They were friends now. *Good* friends. She wouldn't let their friendship be ruined. Then again, if Henry tried to kiss her and she refused, things could get awkward between them. More so than if she just allowed him to do it.

And besides, she sort of *wanted* him to kiss her, right?

As he came in closer, his hands firm over hers, his lips full and ready, Emma realized: she didn't just sort of want him to kiss her. She *really* wanted it, and she wouldn't be able to stop if she tried.

But he didn't do it. "I wanted to show you something," he said. Taking her hands, Henry walked backward to the piano and sat down, guiding her next to him on the bench.

"Don't tell me," she said. "You learned to play something from *Dark Side of the Moon*." She figured it was either that or *Twinkle Twinkle Little Star*.

Henry grinned. "Nope. Better." He cleared his throat and cracked his knuckles, stretching out his fingers. His hands floated onto the keys, and then he began.

Pachelbel. Emma recognized it immediately, and her face lit up. "Whoa! But you don't even play the piano!" she said. "When did you...how did you..." She was completely awestruck looking at him. Tattered jeans, his brown hair like a dirty mop, his lips mouthing along as if the music had words.

Henry kept his head down, his eyes on the keys, swaying his body with the rhythm of the music. A rockstar pianist. The music went on and on, and she could tell he'd made some tweaks here and there, like he was really owning it. Making it his.

As he continued, she closed her eyes and began to sway along with him.

Then something amazing happened. It was like the room was overflowing with *Canon in D*, and Emma couldn't sit there any longer. She got up from the bench and began to dance. No routine. No proper form. No rules. She simply danced, her movements like ribbon trailing behind her.

They continued on for several moments until Henry began to build the tempo. Faster...louder...*harder.* It wasn't Pachelbel anymore. It was something else. Something totally, uniquely Henry. As he played, Emma's body followed suit, twisting and turning, leaping through the air. Her skin burned with the heat. Her sweat dripped to the floor. The room whirled around her, so fast she thought she might collapse right there in the middle of the pulpit, but she knew she couldn't stop. A hundred men couldn't stop her now.

Finally, the racing music began to slow, and a calm fell over the room. Henry's fingers flitted across the keys, easing them both back down. He returned to *Canon in D*, seamlessly, so smooth she could hardly tell how he'd done it. Emma stood sopping wet and breathless in the middle of the pulpit.

When Henry turned to face her again, they just looked at each other, speechless, sucking in air as they tried to catch their breath. After a long moment of gazing, Henry stood up and walked toward her. Without hesitation, he reached out to her and cradled her face in his hands, and his eyes bore into hers.

"I just…had to get it out of my head."

"What?"

"That day, when I first saw you, that's what you were playing, and I haven't stopped picturing that moment." His hands drifted from Emma's cheeks, down to her shoulders, gently around her neck, his fingers tangled up in the longer strands of her hair. "I haven't stopped hearing the music," he said.

Her face relaxed into his hands and she nearly allowed him to do what she knew he wanted to do next, but she came to her senses. She gave him her best *I'm sorry* look as she began. "Henry…"

He placed a finger to her lips. "You know we're good together, Emma. You know this would be great. Why do you keep dismissing me like this? We would be amazing together and you know it."

"I already told you," she said. "I don't have time for a boyfriend. Not now, when I'm already so close. I can't lose focus now."

He took his palms from her face and reached for her hands, then lifted the knot of their fingers and pressed them to his chest. "I won't stop you from dancing. I won't get in the way of your dreams. I just want to be there with you, by your side, every step of the way. Why won't you let me do that?"

"You can be with me," she said, "as my—"

"Friend. Right."

"Can't that be enough for you?"

Henry shook his head slowly, looking at his feet. "I don't understand. If I can be with you as your friend, and spend this much time with you, and we can talk and hang out as much as we do, as friends, why can't we be more?" He gave her that pleading look again. "I want more of you. I want…" His voice faded, then he asked, "What are you really so afraid of?"

To that, Emma didn't know what to say. She *was* afraid. She was so afraid. But of what, she wasn't quite sure.

Henry untangled their hands and cradled her face in his palms again. He leaned in and pressed his lips to hers, but only for a brief moment. Emma allowed him to do so, feeling the swift current of heat that coursed through her body, to the tips of her fingers and toes. She hadn't made note of it right away, but it was the first time she'd ever been kissed.

Like that, anyway.

When Henry pulled away from Emma, he brushed her hair from her face and tried to tuck it behind her ears, but it just fell forward. "You tell me when you're ready," he said, "and until then, I'll be waiting for you, and I'll be the best friend you ever had, for as long as you'll let me. OK? I promise you that."

She thought he might kiss her again, but he didn't. When he turned and left, Emma stood in the middle of the pulpit, the silence heavy around her, the stillness crushing her as she wept.

She wondered, then, how much being with Henry could really get in the way of Juilliard. How much had she wanted to continue on without him, anyway?

Now, alone in her bedroom, as she unraveled the dance that had built up inside her, Emma was sure to have the camera set up on the dresser, facing toward her, recording everything. She was beginning to realize how afraid she was of forgetting again, ever since that day, and that someday this would be a memory too. The feel of the dance. The burn. The release it had given her. She'd gather up her memories now and begin to store them like treasure.

The house was filled with the scent of coffee. Emma danced for nearly half an hour before returning downstairs, setting the camera on the counter in the kitchen. She poured a cup of coffee and sipped it from the sofa in the den, where huge bay windows looked out onto Fifth. She had candles lit around the house and Yo-Yo Ma playing softly in the background. Then, from her father's extensive library, she grabbed a book and read until a calm washed over her again, and she fell asleep to the low music and the flickering candlelight and the breeze that rustled through the curtains in the den.

With rest, Emma knew she wouldn't find peace. Instead she was swallowed up in a nightmare, one that came quick, dragged her into a hellish pit, deep and black. She knew she was dreaming, as she was the last time she'd had this very same dream, though she hadn't been able to force herself out of it. She couldn't thrust herself awake. It was her punishment, Emma thought, for forgetting the day her father died.

The nightmare first came just a few weeks after she moved to Oregon, and she hadn't been sleeping well. She told herself it was because of the night, how the darkness would fall like a heavy blanket, a blackness so rich and thick. It's true what they say: the City never sleeps. The lights never go out, not like they do in Tillamook. It would take a while to get used to the stillness.

That's not really what kept her awake though. What kept her awake was the steady, ceaseless crying from the bedroom next door. Whispered sobs, so soft they could hardly be heard.

One night, after many like this—the crying, the wakefulness—Emma kicked off the covers and walked to the other room. When there was no response to her gentle tapping, she opened the door and entered. It had to have been something like two or three o'clock in the morning.

"Mom," she said.

The bed was immaculately made. Emma's mother was curled up on the window seat, staring at the moon. It was big and full and bright. Emma walked over to her, sat down beside her and rested her head on her shoulder. Her mother had been oddly mute since they first arrived in Oregon, and this moment was no exception. Her eyes remained focused on the moon, glazed over and still.

"I can't sleep either," Emma soothed.

She was surprised when her mother turned toward her, more so when she reached out her hand and cupped Emma's cheek in her palm. Then she nodded slowly and made her way back to bed.

Emma followed her, pulled down the covers and stood by her side as her mother eased herself in, then she walked around and slid in next to her, curling herself against the warmth of the woman's back. She tucked her mother's hair behind her ear.

"There," she said.

When Frances started to whisper, broken mumbles Emma knew weren't directed at her, Emma let the softness of her mother's voice carry her to sleep, though the words she was saying weren't meant to soothe.

Crash. Fire. Fall.

Breathe, Henry. Come back to me.

And that's when the nightmare first sucked her in.

Now, on the second round, it pulled her in deeper until she found herself engulfed in smoke. She felt its stickiness, heavy and clinging, stealing her breath. The heat blazed, wrapping tightly around her, tugging her into its furnace. She saw someone else there, but she could barely make out his face through the heavy smoke and dust. He called out to her, like he'd done before—she could tell by the way he mouthed her name—but just like last time, she couldn't hear his voice.

Then the man rose up, stolen away by the soaring flames. They whipped back at her face, scolding hot. She knew the fall would come; it had ended before with the fall. Emma could feel herself slipping backwards, what felt like a never-ending free fall from a thousand feet up.

If it was going to continue just like before, she knew that with the fall would come the solid, jagged ground below, and she would wake up panting, her hair matted against her face, the pillow damp with sweat and tears.

Her mother next to her, wide-eyed, all of the color drained from her face.

But this time, the fall didn't come. The heat around her continued to build, and the smoke thickened. Something was wrong. It should have been over by now. It should have been less...*real*.

Emma woke up violently, shuddering, still unable to breathe, her skin still burning. She could hear the noise first—a crawling, cackling sound that grew louder as it rushed across the room. Then her eyes registered: *flames*, real ones that lit up the entire room, threatening to surround her.

In a panic, Emma rolled from the sofa and dropped to the floor where she low-crawled across the den to the phone that hung on the wall. It was just on the other side of the room, in the kitchen, but the fire was spreading fast and she had little breath left in her lungs. Struggling, she made it to the kitchen and reached for the phone. She dialed 9-1-1. She could hear the operator answer, but her mind was clouded now, the room spinning around her as the smoke filled her lungs, and try as she might, Emma couldn't respond. She clung to her shirt, holding it over her face as she coughed. With the phone in her other hand, she continued to make her way through the kitchen, toward the front door. She prayed they could hear what was happening over the line.

Before she stepped out, Emma looked back at the flames. Lying across the windowsill in the den, she could just barely see (or had she imagined?) what had started the fire, and what firemen would later confirm: that a candle she'd lit had tipped, its wax dripping to the floor, and as a gust of wind blew

70

through the open window, the flames had fanned against the curtains.

Faintly, Emma could still hear Yo-Yo Ma playing in the background. The music sounded haunting. It would play on loop in her mind for days.

Moments later, the entire house was consumed in the fire and there was nothing Emma could do but stand outside and watch it burn.

CHAPTER 5

They worked for over an hour to put out the flames. Emma sat on a bench at the end of the street, unable to watch, still half-dazed. When it was over, one of the firemen walked toward her and sat down next to her on the bench.

"How bad is it?" she asked without looking at him.

"We don't know the extent of the damage," he said. "Not yet."

"And my neighbors?" Her house was attached to other homes on either side.

"Thankfully we got here quick. The fire was contained to just your home."

Emma sighed in relief. He asked if she had a place to stay, and that's when she finally looked up at him. He was handsome, and not much older than she was. Tall, with thick brown hair and a lean build. He wore a concerned smile as he spoke. Looking at him, Emma couldn't help but think of Henry. Did he ever return to the City? Would he let her stay with him if he had?

Without thinking of it further, she said to the fireman, "Yes, I have a friend in the City. Her name is Chloe Adams. She lives in the Village."

The fireman nodded. "Good," he said. "We'll arrange for transportation." He patted her on the shoulder. "And miss, let me just say, coming from someone who's seen his share of fires…"

"Yes?"

He smiled concernedly again. "All of that back there? It's just stuff."

"Yes," she said, managing a smile as well. "I know."

Chloe stood facing Emma from the kitchen. She looked like an angel, with the yellow glow of sunlight spilling in from the window behind her, a cup of coffee held in each of her hands. "You still drink it black, I hope."

Emma stretched out her arms before sitting up on the sofa in the living room. "Yeah," she said. "I guess some things never change." She cleared a space for Chloe to sit beside her, offering her sincerest smile. Chloe handed her the coffee and watched as Emma inhaled the strong, rich blend she knew Emma had always preferred.

It was the morning after the fire, and they sat together in comfortable silence as Emma looked around the apartment. It wasn't as tidy as she remembered it. There were clothes and knick-knacks strewn about. Pictures hung haphazardly on the wall. Even Chloe seemed less…demure. Less put-together. Her blonde hair was now a mousey shade of brown. Her face and hips were fuller. And in the last ten minutes, she hadn't spoken even once of dancing or Juilliard. That had to be a record.

Halfway finished with her coffee, Emma turned to Chloe. "Everything around here seems different. *You're* different."

"Oh?"

Her face flushed with heat. "Not in a bad way. You just seem more…I don't know…"

"Warm, friendly, inviting?"

"No, I didn't mean—"

Chloe smiled. She sank deeper into the sofa and laid a hand on Emma's knee. "I know. It's true though, I am those things. And everything *has* changed. My home, my family, my dreams."

"How come?"

"Emma, you've been gone a long time. We live in a post-9/11 world now. This is a post-9/11 New York. Nothing will be how it was when you left." She paused before adding, with extra effect, "*Nothing.*"

There it was again. *Post-9/11.* Emma didn't know what to say to that. She knew *she* had changed. Her whole life changed after it happened. But it wasn't long afterward that she'd left the City, and for some reason, in spite of the fear that had risen up in her—or perhaps because of it—Emma imagined that nothing had changed at all.

Chloe interrupted her pondering. "But I see you still do that thing with your lips."

"Oh, right," Emma said, not realizing until now that her bottom lip was folded beneath her fingers. She let go and smiled a little.

"Look, we'll talk more later," Chloe said. "I'll bring you up to speed, and you can tell me what you've been up to for the past three years."

Emma laughed. "That'll be a short conversation on my part."

"Well, for now you should get some sleep. You've been through quite a lot already. Take the whole day to rest, if you'd like. You're gonna need it, because tonight I have a surprise for you."

"Should I be worried?"

Chloe stood from the sofa and looked at Emma with an ornery grin. "A little," she said, and Emma couldn't help but smile. "Do you need anything?"

"Just the basics. A towel, some toiletries. That sort of thing."

"Yeah, sure."

"And something to write on, if you have."

Chloe returned to the kitchen and searched, digging out a spiral notepad and a mechanical pencil from one of the drawers. "Will this work?"

Emma's smile widened. "Perfect," she said.

It's a cool Saturday morning in October. I had so many memories recorded already, but the camera is gone along with everything else that burned in the fire. So for now, pencil and paper will have to do.

Chloe's apartment is eclectic and cozy. It almost reminds me of my grandmother's house in Tillamook. Since the fire, Augusta's house is the only real home I have left, and I'm starting to miss it.

I remember when Lois and I first arrived in Oregon. It took some getting used to, but Augusta was warm and welcoming and so easy to talk to. She'd just remarried, and in spite of the rumors, it was hard not to like Charles. It was hard not to like the way he made her smile.

I remember one morning, cuddled in the warmth of the sofa in the den, Augusta and I sat together watching through big windows as the sun rose across the farm, flitting up the spaces between the mountains in glorious strands of pink and purple and red.

I turned to Augusta. "Do you love him?" I asked. She sat quietly sipping her tea, not yet ready to answer my question.

Then, finally, she said, "Sweetheart, I wouldn't have married him if I didn't love him."

"You know what I mean. Do you love him, you know, like you loved—"

"Your grandfather? Yes, I love him very much like I loved your grandfather. I love him fully as my husband, and that means I love him as

my companion, as my partner and my lover and, well…as my best friend."

"You know what people are saying though, right?"

"If by people you mean your mother, then yes. And yes, I know exactly what was said. That I'm getting older now and I've settled, simply because I'm lonely. I'll admit it was a daunting idea, the thought of growing old by myself, but it didn't consume me. After all, you're only as old as you feel, right? Now, I know I'm no spring chicken, but my dear, I'm still a woman and I still have some fight in me, ya know. I still have needs.*"*

"Augusta!"

"Oh, Emma. One of these days you really will need to lighten up."

"I'm sure of it," I said. "But I really wanted to know, you know, about the other thing people are saying. About how it's like you just…moved on. Did you forget about him, then? Were you really able to move on from him?"

I can still remember verbatim the words that followed. I'd let the little monologue replay over and over in my head, singing along to the cadence of Augusta's words as if to memorize them, as if they held a truth I'd really need to hear again someday.

"Emma, let me tell you. You will never move on from one of your true loves. Your grandfather was my first love, the great love of my life, and I have no intention of moving on from him, and Charles knows that. But what can he do?"

She paused, taking another slow sip of tea, and the silence grew awkward. I thought she might have been waiting for me to respond, but what was I supposed to say? I opened my mouth to let out a simple "I don't know" but Augusta continued before I could speak.

"Nothing, is what. I will never forget your grandfather. He has my heart, my whole heart, but now so does Charles. And that's OK, Em. It's OK. I know it won't make much sense to you. You're young, and it shouldn't have to make sense to you now. I'm sure you can't begin to imagine having to share your heart in this way. You can't imagine that one day, after you've given your whole heart to someone, that they will be gone from you. Then you will have to pick yourself up, piece yourself back together until you're intact, wholly you again, and if you happen to find another who is worth your whole heart, you let them have it. You let them have all of it, entirely. Oh, I know it doesn't make sense to you now. I know you can't imagine what it must be like to have a broken heart be whole again, the way I have. But one day you may have to, Em. One day you may have to find love, and then find love again."

I sat quietly for a long while, staring pensively across the room. "I can't," I finally said. "I really can't imagine."

PART TWO

CHAPTER 6

It's an all-day train ride from Atlanta, Georgia to New York City, but Henry doesn't mind. Figures he'll crack open a book and read, pick at his guitar for a bit, maybe find a stranger to chat with. And when he grows bored with those things, he'll just sit in the quiet and stare out the window, out at the landscape that starts to dip and roll and wave ahead, an invitation for him to *keep on truckin'*—and a devious invitation at that, because he knows the ride is about to get rougher. He knows the mountains are just ahead.

Henry also has some idea, for the most part, what he'll be going home to. That his mom will have the house sparkling clean by the time he arrives; that she'll be happy and anxious to see him. But there'll be something else, too. This visit will be bittersweet for her (maybe more bitter than sweet) since it'll be the last of his visits home for quite a long time.

Twelve months gone, and that's if they don't get extended.

Not that she didn't handle the first deployment well. She did quite well, actually, remaining strong not just for her sake (and not just for Tabby's, either), but for Henry's sake too. But he's no idiot. He knows what's coming, and all it entails: The Second Deployment. The *here we go again.*

Everyone keeps saying how second deployments are harder than first deployments. For soldiers, for families. What, you think the second round is gonna make this whole thing easier? Because they know what to expect? Like, *been there, done that?* Don't be so naïve. He knows what second deployments mean; they all do. Second deployments mean this thing is still going, mean it's all a routine now (and *that's* when you know you're really in trouble), mean the odds are now doubly stacked against them.

At the very least, Henry tells himself, he hadn't been called to Baghdad on the dry run. But he's a veteran now. He's ready. Ready as he'll ever be.

The train is quieter than he expected. It makes him feel uneasy. So many people, all sitting stoically, their voices hushed, staring out their respective windows. It's worse that he's here in his army uniform, that he sticks out like a sore thumb. A big, green thumb. All eyes on him. He didn't have time to change though. Sergeant Davis kept him late because, apparently, *Henry doesn't listen.* And, you know, because he *can*, so why the hell not?

They were buddies, Henry and Sergeant Davis, back before the first deployment when they were both just a couple of lowly privates. Went through basic training together. Shared a room. Hell, they even *cuddled* for a bit. (Don't judge, man. Afghanistan gets *cold*, and sometimes body heat is all you got.)

Sergeant Davis is a tall burly guy, dark dark dark. I'm talking skin, eyes, hair. He's a big, dark guy, and he's a real good listener too. He's strong, smart, an outstanding soldier, but that's not what he's got going for him. It's the listening. Sergeant Davis can follow *orders*, and *that's* how you get promoted.

That also happens to be the thing Henry is worst at.

So last night, this newbie soldier does something totally stupid and reckless. He's nineteen, just got back from basic training, and what does he do? He hitches a ride with a couple of guys to some bar or strip club or something like that, twenty minutes off post. Those guys stay out all night, way past the break of dawn, and come six o'clock this newbie soldier is still somehow wasted, and *alone*. His buddies ditched him hours earlier.

Henry gets the call at 6:02. First formation is at *6:40.*

If this guy's late, he's in deep shit. He's still in uniform, which means he's been drinking…*in uniform.* Plus he's underage. Plus, and here's the real biggie: he's gonna be late. To *first formation.* At least he'll be dressed.

Of course Henry is the one he calls. Henry is the guy who doesn't drink or gamble or bring girls back to the barracks. He has a license and a car and a credit card. He's the responsible one. The *adult.* It's sort of hilarious, actually. So why is Henry the one always getting in trouble? Because he can't say no. This kid has readied himself for the perfect storm, and Henry can't let him get in that kind of trouble. He *should*, but he can't.

Henry picks up the phone. "Where are you?" he asks. The kid tells him. "Be there in ten," Henry says. It's a rough estimate. He'll be there in fifteen, if he's lucky. If they're *both* lucky.

So, he gets there, and just like he said, the kid's already dressed. He leaps into Henry's car and they fly off. They make it back on post by 6:25, and the kid's standing in formation (a little loopy, but at least he's in uniform) by 6:30. Right on time.

It's common knowledge in the army: If you're ten minutes early, you're on time. If you're on time, *you're late.* (If you're late, it's unacceptable.) The kid's on time but unlike him, Henry is *not* dressed. He has ten minutes to get back to the barracks, dress and shave, and make it to first formation…just to be considered "late."

Shit.

He stands in place at 6:42, right after hearing the 1st sergeant as he calls out "Form up." His chest sinks. The entire company knows he's late. He can hear them cat-calling as he walks up. "Ooooooh."

I'm gonna kill that kid.

Here's how it works: the army has this thing called "Chain of Command" (maybe you've heard of it?) and it really is like this big metaphorical chain. Whoever's at the bottom gets whipped the most. So 1st sergeant, he's sort of at the top here, he whips the chain down at the platoon sergeant who then, pissed off, gives a good whipping to the squad leader. *Henry's* squad leader: Sergeant Davis.

Sergeant Davis does not like to be whipped by this chain. Especially on account of Henry—again.

He considers Henry's punishment. Two minutes of unacceptable lateness. What shall we do, what shall we do? Pushups? Nah, Henry's too strong for pushups to really *hurt* anymore (lots of practice). He deserves something worse. Something grueling. Henry can see in his eyes: he's about to get smoked.

Davis, former buddy of his, takes his sweet time thinking up a good punishment for Henry. At the end of the day, once everyone else has already signed out for the weekend, he calls him over. "Barracks cleanout," he says.

Henry's eyes widen. "Sir, my train leaves in an hour."

Davis gives a sort of grimace. "Well then, you better get moving."

Barracks cleanout means Henry has to take everything out of his second-floor room and carry it all downstairs. I'm talking clothes, dishes, *furniture*. Everything. Then he has to carry it all back up. In *full uniform*. It takes a half an hour, and Henry is officially late for the train. He's almost late for the one after that.

When he's finally done serving his pointless punishment, Henry gives Davis *the look*. You know, *with his eyes*: *I can't believe you, man. I can't believe what you've become.* Now, I know what you're thinking, you women who are reading this: *How does Henry know about* the look? Like it's some big secret.

Because, ladies, let me tell you: Henry grew up with three women. *Three.* His mom, his sister, his niece. The look was always the same, even coming from the littlest of them: his niece, Tabby. It's like they're born with it or something. All women. Pre-programmed. Now, Henry is not a very good listener, but he does learn quickly. *Believe that.*

Sergeant Davis must have had some experience in this area as well, because you know what he does after Henry gives him *the look*? He drops his head, drops it real low, into his chest, as he strolls up next to Henry. Then he puts his hand on Henry's shoulder and says, his voice all steady and calm, defeated, "I went easy on you this time, Hayes. I'm just lookin' out for you." Which is probably only partly true.

When will Henry *learn* to *listen*? It can't be easy for Davis to have to keep on disciplining him like this. Can it?

As Henry sits here, letting it stew, he takes out his journal and jots some things down.

Yeah, his *journal*. You heard me right. Now let me explain, because I don't want you getting the wrong idea, but if you're gonna know Henry, you've got to know everything. So here it is:

He keeps a journal. A small one, pocket-sized. Olive green, plain. Very masculine, OK? And he uses it to write down his thoughts. Nothing elaborate. He doesn't promise to write in it every day, and he doesn't begin with *Dear Diary* or anything superfluous like that. He likes to think of it as a *record of thoughts*, a way to unwrap some things that seem to go on in his brain on their accord, to work through them in a way that makes sense. To *figure himself out*. So he can move on and get to fixing whatever it is that's wrong.

But also, he keeps a journal because he *likes* it. The way the words bleed out of him, the look of them on paper. He's a writer. It's one of those embarrassing things he never tells anyone. He didn't grow up with a dad around, but he knows if he had one his dad would say something to Henry like: *Real men don't keep journals.* Like they probably don't write sappy love songs, either, and then sing to themselves as they strum a guitar—alone in their rooms. They probably don't sit on the train and wonder where everyone else is going, all the journeys that lie ahead, paying no mind to the lovely stewardess with the cleavage that spills from her blouse. (There's only ever been one girl for him. It's worse than being gay, his fake-dad would have said.) Real men don't keep thinking about some girl from high school whenever they stumble back into their hometown.

Hometown. Really, that's what he's gonna start calling New York City now? The question comes and goes. He shrugs.

It always surprises Henry, the moments he thinks of his dad—whoever he is, wherever he is, whatever the hell he's doing. It hits him now, as he sits on the train, his guitar on his lap, his journal spread open on the table in front of him, pen in hand. He's about to write something ridiculous (*on my way back home again, maybe I'll see her this time*), but just as the tip of his pen touches the paper, Henry hears a familiar voice. He stares at the tiny blue dot as the voice says, *Really, son? This again?* And then something about learning to be a *real* man. Like some broken record.

He almost gets angry, but then he doesn't. It's fun, being an adult like that. Being mature and stuff. *I was gonna do something stupid, but then I just didn't.* Apparently his dad never got that lesson. He must have never really grown up.

So as he sits here, *not getting angry,* he thinks of him. *Dad.* And his whole fake tirade about real men and journals. (He'd probably use the word "diary" though, just to drive it in further. Henry's insignificance to him. How he'll never measure up.) Henry smiles when he thinks of what he would say in return.

I put on this uniform every damned day. I wear boots to work, and a helmet, and a bullet-proof vest. I spent twelve months in Afghanistan. I send money home to Mom (remember her?) every month, even when she says she doesn't need it. I've slept in mud, gone months without even a pillow at night, carried a hundred pounds on my back for hours, days. In the blazing heat. In the freezing cold. I've taken a bullet, Dad, so tell me: what the hell have you ever done?

Tell me, what the hell kind of man are you?

Henry looks down at his journal and smiles. He's written the whole thing down, his little diatribe, and he's oddly OK with his smugness. A second later though, Henry tears the sheet from the journal and crumples it up.

"More coffee, sir?" A soft but high-pitched voice interrupts his moment. He looks up at the stewardess, bent over just enough so he'll get a good look at her chest, her big blue eyes sparkling like diamonds.

He slides his mug toward her and nods.

She eyes his uniform as she pours. "So, are you…going? Or coming back?"

"Going," he says. "Just a few more days."

"Oh, you poor thing." She hands him back the mug, now full to the brim.

"It's not so bad," Henry tells her, and he actually believes, for the smallest second, that he hasn't just lied to this girl.

At half past eight, Henry is greeted with the smell of

flowers and fresh air as it blows through the open windows. The fading rays of twilight barely break through the panes, shadows cast throughout the apartment. It's stunning, really. Everything seems so much bigger and warmer and brighter, every time he returns. As far off from the grimy barracks in Atlanta as black is from white.

"Henry, you're home," his mom says with her delicate smile, her arms stretching slowly out toward him as she walks in from the balcony.

It's the first time he notices visible evidence of her growing older. She's barely fifty, but already her waist and face and hair have thinned. Her eyes have turned a milky-blue. How much harder has the last year been for her than what she's let on? First the news of his second deployment, then his sister...

But still she's graceful as ever. Radiant.

"Hey, Mom," he says. "The place looks great. *You* look great."

"Oh, Henry." She blushes, then pulls him into a hug and kisses him on the cheek. She cradles his face in her soft, tiny hands, and examines him thoroughly. Henry can see in her eyes exactly what she's thinking, what she always thinks after these long stretches of his absence: *My little boy, so grown up.*

"Let me see if Tabitha's awake," she says.

Henry watches as she turns and practically floats down the hall. It's just the three of them now. Mom, Tabby, Henry. It's still strange for him to think that his sister and her husband passed away just a year ago, not long after he returned home from his first tour in Afghanistan. *Tour*, like it was some kind of vacation. A sightseeing trip. Like he'd come home with a T-shirt that said: *My son went to Afghanistan and all I got was this lousy T-shirt.* (That wasn't funny.) It's strange for him to think that more time hasn't gone by since the accident.

Not that he can call what happened an accident. Was it any accident that the other driver and his friends had gone drinking that night? Was it any accident that they decided to go for a joy ride out to the shore right afterward? It was no accident, as far as Henry was concerned. It was murder in cold blood.

But if there was one little blessing that came out if it all, it was Tabitha. Eric and Laura had left little Tabby, six years old now, with Henry and his mom. Well, legally just with his mom, but Tabby soon became more like a daughter to him than a niece. It's more like she is a *part* of him now, something as vital to his existence as air or water or love.

"Henry!" her mousey, sweet little voice calls out as she runs toward him. Her pigtails are a wreck and her nightgown disheveled as she drags her same old worn-out purple teddy bear down the hall. He can't believe how much taller she's gotten, and man, is she starting to look like Laura.

"Tabby cat," he says. Her small arms wrap around his neck.

"Did you miss me?"

"More than anything," she squeals back.

"I brought something for you." Henry unwraps himself from her arms and pulls out a bag of cookies, each shaped and patterned like tiny flags outlined with waves on the sides as if they're actually flying high, flapping away in the breeze.

Mom glances at Henry, amused but questioning. "Sorry," he tells her. "I couldn't resist."

"Oh no, don't apologize." She turns to Tabby. "It would be a good idea to save them for after dinner though, don't you think, Tabitha?"

"Not really," she says, sounding disappointed but at the same time quite mature. "I guess I can be OK with that though."

A while later, after they've had dinner and tucked Tabitha into bed, Henry sits on the sofa, his arms pretzeled behind his head, his feet up on the coffee table, one foot over the other. His mom walks into the living room.

"So, tell me everything," he says. He motions to the empty space next to him on the sofa.

"What are you still doing here?"

"I thought we'd talk. Like we always do."

"No…you *always* play at the bar your first night back in the

City."

"Yeah, but this time is different."

She seems to relent as she sits down next to him. "Henry, this is not the first time we're going through this. You're going to be fine, and so are we."

"You don't know that. I just…"

She pats him on the shoulder and leans into him with a kiss on the cheek. "Go. Don't disappoint your fans. You know they'd miss you more than we will."

Henry manages a smile. "I don't believe that."

"Good," she says. "It was a horrible joke." Then she stands up from the sofa and walks away, just like that, leaving a cup of coffee untouched on the table in front of him.

"Night, Mom," Henry says.

She stops in front of her bedroom door and glances back at him. Her hair, a sheet of blonde now streaked with gray, falls across her shoulder. In the delicate way she always does, she smiles. "Goodnight, son."

CHAPTER 7

I don't know who our friendship had been harder on, me or Henry. He never had a problem telling me when I was acting like a stuck-up bitch, and he was right about that most of the time. But Henry wasn't an angel either. He was inappropriate, stubborn and immature, and I was the one to tell him he needed to grow up. He wasn't in Albuquerque anymore. He was in the big leagues now, and it was time he started acting like it.

Our first big fight ensued that one summer we spent together as friends. With school only three days a week for us in the summer semester at Academy, we spent nearly every day together, but that didn't stop me from attending practices and recitals during my summer off-days. I was still consumed with dance, but Henry had nothing to keep him busy. He messed around on his guitar now and then, and I'd see him writing songs of his own from time to time, but other than that, I was it for him. By mid-summer, after all that time together, we were fighting nearly every day.

The problem was this. We would both be entering our senior year at Academy in just a couple more months, and Henry hadn't planned for anything beyond high school. It infuriated me! When I was a freshman, I already had the next ten years of my life planned out, down to the tiniest details. Meanwhile, there Henry was, with no idea what he wanted to do with his life. He had hopeless dreams of doing something big with his guitar and his songs, and he'd go on and on about that sometimes, but that just made me angrier. In my mind, he had no chance of making it big that way. Not from where he came from. His humble beginnings. He'd have to plan for something more practical.

And so I berated him over the issue, probably too much, and for the most part he just sort of took it. Until one day, we were sitting down at a little restaurant in Brooklyn, and his switch flipped. He just blew up about it.

"Aren't you freaked out?" I asked him for probably the hundredth time. "Most of the students in our class have already submitted their applications and scheduled auditions. Any decent school in the northeast will want to have it by now, and especially with your background—"

He hadn't been keeping eye contact with me, but to this he darted his face toward me, his eyes dark and cold, filled with hurt. "My background?"

For the first time since we'd become friends, I was embarrassed to have thought of him like that. Our social differences were unspoken before, but now that I'd released them in the air around us, there was no taking it back. "No, I didn't...I mean, I don't...I just..."

Henry held the palm of his hand up in front of me. "Stop it, Emma," he said. "I get it."

I get it. I knew what that really meant. That I wasn't just acting like a stuck-up bitch this time. I was a bitch.

"Henry, I..." I didn't know what to say. There was no saving myself from this one. "I'm sorry," was all I could manage. I thought that would be enough. With Henry, that was usually enough.

Not this time. He slammed his drink down on the table. When he spoke again, his voice was raised. Loud and steady.

"What the hell do you care, anyway? It's not like it will affect you. It's not like I'll ever see you again after graduation. So what's it to you? Or do you just like telling me what to do with my life?" His eyes bore into mine. "Is that it, you want to fix me or something? Make me into someone I'm not? Are you ashamed of me? Tell me, Emma. What is it? Why the hell do you give a damn about me and my future?"

Before I could answer, Henry reached into his wallet and threw a twenty on the table, then he turned away and stormed out of the restaurant, leaving me alone to wallow in my stupidity.

In a rush, I threw a couple extra bucks on the table for tip and ran after Henry. When I found him, he was leaning over the railing on the Brooklyn Promenade, facing out toward lower Manhattan. I walked up to him and stood by his side, allowing him to glower at me with that spiteful expression on his face. "I'm really sorry," I said again.

Henry shook his head and turned away from me, toward the City.

"You don't have to say anything, but just hear me out, OK?"

He turned around and leaned his back against the railing. He looked at me expectantly, but said nothing.

I stood in front of him and held both of his hands in mine. "I don't want to change you, and I'm certainly not ashamed of you. But I do care about you, and I care about your future. You're my best friend and I don't want to lose you. OK, Henry? I don't want to lose what we have. So please, please, can you forgive me?"

He breathed out and nodded a little. "I guess," he said unconvincingly. But I was convinced.

"You guess?"

"Yeah," he said. "Sure."

"So...we're friends again?"

Henry gave a wan smile. "Yeah, we're friends. But just so you know, that was the most fucked up thing you ever said to me, and I swear that if you ever pull that shit again—"

"I know, Henry. I know.*"*

He wrapped his arms around me in a friendly, almost brotherly hug, and with my cheek pressed against his chest I looked up at him again.

"About what you said before, about not seeing each other after you graduate..."

"Right," he said with a laugh. Then he combed his hands through my hair and planted a kiss on my forehead. "Like you could get rid of me that easy."

• • •

Henry's favorite stage was always this one, this small stage in the corner of a bar on the Upper West Side, and he can't help but notice what a favorite he is here too. He's got just a few fans but they're pretty loyal, because as soon as they find out he's on leave from the army and scheduled to play, the whole place books up. All 450 square feet of it.

It's an intimate joint, casually trendy, perfect for the bluesy, jazzy, coffeehouse-style music he plays. The audience consists of mostly hipsters, young artists and intellectuals. Writers and dancers and theater junkies. All locals, no doubt. It's little more than a stone's throw from Central Park but tucked away just enough so the tourists can't find it and fill up the place. He's heard people say it's the best kept secret in Manhattan. He's heard people say that he is.

Henry takes his seat in the center of the stage, just him and his guitar. The room fills with a smoky haze and the lights dim. He can barely see his own hand in front of him, but he can hear the roar of the crowd. He can feel the energy building around him.

And every time he starts to play, when his fingers strum down across the strings, he thinks of Emma. Does she think of him too? Did she stay in the City long after everything happened? And might she, one day, just by chance, stumble into this bar on the same night Henry is scheduled to play?

• • •

It wasn't much. The air was sticky with smoke and that grainy smell of beer, and the people looked like characters in a play. Who knows, maybe they were? It was small and crowded and loud. As Chloe ushered her in, Emma felt hesitantly optimistic. It wasn't what she expected for her first night out. Why had Chloe brought her here? And was she really ready for more surprises?

"What is this place?"

"Your surprise," Chloe said.

"What, you're gonna get me drunk?"

"Yeah." Chloe grinned. "Something like that."

With her hand gently clasped around Emma's arm, Chloe led her to the center of the room. She turned to Emma and said, "Wait here while I get us some drinks. Jack and Coke?"

Even after a full day's rest, Emma felt sleepy but her lips feigned a smile. "Vodka Cranberry."

"Oh." Chloe smiled and gave a little nod. "Look who's all grown up."

Emma stood alone then, glancing around the room, still wondering why Chloe brought her here but telling herself she'd play along. Be a good friend. Go through the motions. Whatever it would take to get through the night.

The lights overhead began to dim, and a steady rumble coursed through the crowd. A man walked onto the stage, dark and emo-looking, with gangly limbs and thick-rimmed, oversized glasses. His jeans looked tighter than Emma's. Apparently he was there to announce the evening's performer, but it seemed the crowd already knew.

Chloe strode up beside Emma and placed the bright red drink in her hand as the man's voice whined. "Ladies and gents, without further ado, give it up for Henry Hayes!"

Henry Hayes? *Oh my god.* And just like that, Emma was back in that narrow Academy hallway, with the bright lights overhead, her eyes filled up with tears, and Henry's hand was reaching out toward her. *Actually, it's Henry,* he'd said. The name had flowed from his lips like silk. Her *father's* name.

But this time the name didn't land on her ears so gently; it crashed into them.

"*Surprise,*" Chloe whispered in her ear. Emma jumped, crumbling out of her frozen state, her heart slamming against her chest. The drink was shaking in her hand.

"I thought he…moved," she managed to say. "Back to Albuquerque."

Chloe looked disbelievingly at Emma. "*That's* the last you heard?"

"Yeah. Why?" And how could Chloe have thought this was a good idea…bringing Emma here, without any notice? She looked down at her faded jeans, her long tangled hair falling in front of her face, and she found herself wishing she'd spent more time getting ready.

Chloe was shaking her head. "He never said anything to me about Albuquerque. All I remember is him joining the army."

She must have read the bewildered look on Emma's face. "Oh, you mean…you didn't know?"

"What? The army? *Henry*? No, I had no idea!"

Chloe continued nonchalantly, looking up at the stage as Henry walked across it. "Yeah, like, three years ago. His mom still lives here though, and when he comes home on leave, he plays. Always the same old stuff. Always at this bar."

Emma nodded and took a sip from her drink. It suddenly felt so slippery in her hand, she thought she might drop it. "I guess more things have changed around here than I thought."

"Yeah," Chloe said. "I guess so."

Emma watched Henry intently, knowing he couldn't see her. He was bigger now, stronger-looking, darkly tanned. His jaw was sharper than it was when he left, his cheekbones higher, his arms sculpted. His long hair was cut short, but still he was the same old Henry. With that cheeky grin of his, those chocolate-brown, almond eyes. The way he held the guitar in his hands, strung across his chest.

As his fingers played over the strings, Emma felt the familiar sound. *Felt* it. And her mind was taken back to what used to be their favorite little coffeehouse on a shaded corner in DUMBO—Down Under the Manhattan and Brooklyn Overpass—where she and Henry would sit and talk for hours. He'd bring his guitar, anxious to show her what he'd been working on, and she'd just kick her feet up and listen, cradling a latté in her hand, nearly falling asleep to the sounds of him strumming, the birds and the wind and the endless gathering of people that bustled by.

She opened her eyes and let out her breath, wondering how long she'd had them closed, wondering how long she'd been holding it in.

• • •

He never thought it would actually happen, but just in case, Henry scans the crowd. It's too difficult to see at first, with the smoke machines on full-blast, but between sets, that's when he does it. That's when he has a look around.

There's the goth girl in the back who always wears costume wings. The big scruffy guy with the unlit pipe. A man with a cape. Chloe, Emma's friend from high school, who he'll talk to afterward. She stands as she always does, quiet and smiling, just here for support, with a drink in her hand.

And then, *there she is.* Standing next to Chloe, her copper hair falling past her shoulders, her skin a soft, pale, creamy white. Her eyes—he remembers them well. Bright, green, piercing. And her lips are painted red.

"*Emma.*" The faces in the crowd look up at him curiously. The room is silent as they wait.

Then he hears the winged goth girl as she shouts from across the room. "Who's Emma?"

Oh fuck, he said it out loud. And *oh, double fuck*, the mic is still hot.

Henry watches as Emma's face turns red, her green eyes open wide. She looks at Chloe and hands off her drink. After she shoots him one last glance, she turns around and walks out.

And just like that, she is gone from him—again.

• • •

Emma waited outside until Chloe came running out of the bar, searching for her. She was standing at the corner beneath the little pool of light from the streetlamp, her arms crossed over her chest.

"What the hell happened in there?" Chloe said.

Emma looked up at Chloe and the tears she'd been holding back started to tumble, unwillingly, streaming heavy black lines of mascara down her cheeks. The knot tightened in the back of her throat. How could she explain her reaction to Chloe? Could she explain it to herself? Her voice trembled as she spoke. "He saw me," she said.

"Yeah, *and?*"

She couldn't tell by Chloe's expression if she was confused, or if perhaps she was angry with her now. Disappointed, maybe, that her plan hadn't played out so smoothly.

"*And...*" Emma stammered. "Why on Earth did you bring me here? What the hell were you thinking!"

Yes, Chloe was definitely angry now, her face a bright crimson red, the little veins in her temples growing larger, pulsing. But her voice was more evenly patient than Emma expected. She hated that.

"I was thinking that it's Henry," Chloe said. "You know, Henry Hayes. He was only, like, your *best friend* at Academy."

"What? *You* were my best friend."

"Emma, let's be serious now. I was a bitch in high school. And you two were practically a couple. Fucking inseparable."

With the backside of her hand, Emma wiped the tears from her face. "I know. But all that changed."

"Yeah, I can see that. So what was it? Come on, Em. Time to fess up."

Emma hesitated, but just briefly. She looked up at Chloe and smiled. Her friend. Her *best* friend. She choked back her ridiculous sobs and nodded. "Fine, I'll tell you what happened. Just...not here."

Emma reached for Chloe's hand and led her to the corner booth of an old diner in Midtown. The air was cool and the noisy, crowded streets made it so much easier not to talk along the way. It was a perfect walk to calm her nerves.

A half hour later, they were sitting across from one another. Over stale fries and burnt coffee, Emma managed to tell her everything. What happened, how it had ended, why she hadn't seen or heard from Henry since.

CHAPTER 8

Three years earlier

It had taken the usual three hours to get ready. Emma pinned her hair up tightly, caked her face with layer upon layer of heavy makeup. She sucked in, squeezing into a leotard. It fit her lean figure beautifully. With her hair and makeup done, she looked at herself in the mirror, at her near-perfect reflection.

At seventeen, you'd think she would have loved all the fuss that went into recitals. Getting dolled up, being the center of attention. But she hated it, actually. She hated looking in the mirror at the reflection of a stranger, that girl with all the makeup and glitter. She hated the screaming fights with her mother as she pulled on Emma's hair, tugged at her cheeks, told her to suck it in just…a little…more. She hated the smell of aerosol and the perfume that would linger for days.

There was one thing though: Emma loved performing. From backstage she could hear her name announced, the gentle build of the crowd that followed. She stepped onto the stage, the lights blinding, darkness blanketing everyone's faces. In this shadowed place, she could see nothing but light, could hear nothing but the first notes of music that began to play, as a hush fell over the room.

My, what heaven must be like, she thought.

Emma performed the dance flawlessly, just as she always did. It was like she could actually *feel* the music. Or more so, it was like she was the one creating it. As if, with every movement of her body, the music itself was emanating from within her.

It was a rather boring number, to be honest. It was always that way with the introductions. That's what this was, Emma's first recital of her senior year, her introduction as a dance major to the entire Academy community. The school was showing her off here. No, the school was showing itself off. "Look how well we've taught her! Look at the talent we've created!" It was less for Emma than it was for them. So it had to be boring. It had to be far easier than what she was capable of doing. Because really, it had to be perfect.

When it was over, Emma stood breathless, her heart drumming as she scanned the crowd. She spotted her parents and her professors, all beaming politely. No one stood—as it would have been tacky, by Academy's standards—but the applause went on and on until she imagined everyone's hands had gone raw and red from the incessant slapping.

She looked for Henry among the crowd, but just as she thought she might have seen him, the roses were showered onto her. It was as if they were raining upwards from the audience. The fresh, flowery aroma filled the room. There was

no way she could find him now, what with the torrential up-
pour. So she stopped trying. She curtsied low, smiling brightly,
and allowed the audience to drown her in its praise.

A reception followed backstage. It was a boring, stuffy
party, meant to celebrate the accomplishments of Emma and
the other artists who had performed that night. But she felt
invisible, as if she hadn't *just* graced the stage, since no one
even seemed to notice her presence.

The backstage area had been transformed into a ballroom.
Intricate tapestries draped the velvet-lined walls. Glass
chandeliers hung from the ceiling. A jazz band played in the
corner. There was champagne too, offered even to the minors
in attendance. A toast was made in honor of the Academy and
the performers.

Noticing her parents on the other side of the room
socializing with the higher-ups (including the dean of the
school, and *was that a recruiter?),* Emma took just a tiny sip of
the bubbly before setting the glass back down. What Academy
tolerated, her parents did not always.

She walked toward them but stopped after she caught her
mother's eyes, offering a look she had learned to know well:
Not now, dear. We'll talk later. Her father gave a knowing, patient
smile.

There were at least five other introductions in attendance.
A pianist, a cellist, an actor. Another dancer, though she hadn't

compared to Emma in skill or style or delivery. They were easy to spot, since they were the only people in the room who looked anywhere near her age. She looked for Henry too. He should have been easy to find at a party like this. But there was still no sight of him. She thought for sure he'd show up tonight, so where the hell was he?

The other dancer approached her. A rich, posh girl from England. *Old money.* "Emma!" she called.

Emma was surprised the girl knew her name. She fluttered toward her, every movement a dance even when she wasn't onstage. "We're all headed out to dinner," the girl said. "A celebration of sorts. Care to join us?"

Emma didn't, actually. Not in the least. Besides, it wasn't time to celebrate anything yet. Not until she was accepted to Juilliard. And anyway, Henry could still show up and she'd want to be here when he did.

"No thanks," she said. "I have plans to meet with a friend."

The girl rolled her eyes. "That Henry guy?" With her hand on Emma's elbow, the girl pulled her aside and lowered her voice. "Emma, let's think seriously now. You know what everyone is saying about him, right? He doesn't belong here, you know that. He doesn't fit in here. He's gonna ruin your reputation."

Reputation. It seemed, sometimes, that was more important

than effort or skill. Emma knew she should have defended him then, but she didn't. "No, I'm not waiting for Henry. I'm waiting for a friend of mine. An old friend. You don't know her." She swallowed hard, engulfed in shame.

Posh-girl nodded suspiciously. "Well, all right then. I guess we'll see you around." On her dainty toes, she darted away from Emma and rejoined the group. The pianist—a tall, gangly guy with jet black hair and skin whiter than Emma's. The cellist—small and blonde, her pointy little nose tipped upward. The actor—a carrot top, heavy-set, with a belly that stuck out farther than his rear. And the posh girl, she could've been taken for Emma's sister: tall and thin and graceful.

It was true what the girl had said, that Henry didn't fit in at Academy. But in so many ways, neither did Emma. No matter who or what she happened to look like.

Standing alone now, her sweaty fingers tangled up together and messing around with her lower lip again, Emma decided to give up on Henry. He wouldn't be there, and she couldn't jump to conclusions about why he hadn't come. Maybe something happened to him. Maybe she should have been *worried*, not angry. But she couldn't find it in her to be either.

She walked back over to her mother and tapped her on the shoulder.

"Mom," she said, her voice just above a whisper.

Nothing.

"Momma," she said again.

The woman swatted her away with a thin hand through the air. In a louder voice, Emma said, "I'm leaving now. I'll see you back home."

She nodded then, somewhat in Emma's direction. "Yes, yes. That's fine." Who could be sure she was talking to Emma? Her parents were so lost in conversation now, even her father hadn't acknowledged her.

Emma snaked her way through the crowd and left. She stepped outside and felt the cool air envelop her. She was hardly dressed for an outing, and she wasn't even sure where she wanted to go. If Henry had been there, they'd walk around the City together, discuss the pompousness of the evening. Maybe they'd go for coffee or ice cream or hail a cab to anywhere. Henry was good for stuff like that.

The neighborhoods that surrounded Academy were quieter than most, and for Emma, on this night especially, the silence was refreshing. Wearing a light jacket, shorts and ballet flats, her duffel bag slung across her shoulder, she strolled aimlessly. A few blocks north, a few blocks west, a few more south, then back east. What was probably several miles later, she had come full-circle and was near the Academy again.

It was a relatively small school, hidden amongst row after row of old brownstones. Emma explored, something she

110

seldom had time to do, until she stumbled upon a wide alleyway that offered an inspiring view. Fresh laundry strung across the alley; potted plants adorned the balconies; a dog was barking in the distance.

She walked the length of the alley, then back. She sat down on the pavement, leaning her back against the wall, her legs straight out in front of her. She looked up at the windows above, able to make out the faintest bits of conversation. A father and son bonding over a football game; two girlfriends in the heat of an argument—something about a guy, it seemed; a couple making love.

Her smile grew wide before clearing away as she thought about all of the people out there, some coming together, others pulling apart. She was glad not to have that stress in her life, having kept everyone—her friends and even her family, more often than not—at arm's length. But then, she sometimes wondered, what was the point of it all? She tried to picture her life after Juilliard. Would she be rich? Famous? Dancing on Broadway? Or would she praise God it was over, thankful to finally live her life?

Just as quickly as the thought had entered her mind, it faded. Emma slid the duffel bag from her shoulder and set it against the wall, then stretched her arms out in front of her, touching her fingers to her toes, tummy to thighs. She inhaled deeply before rising up again, reaching her hands above her head. Deep, steady breaths. She slipped off her shoes and rose to her feet.

Standing, Emma pointed and flexed her feet out in front of her, one at a time, rotating her toes around her ankles. Then, with her feet flat on the pavement, her inner thighs nearly touching, Emma rolled back and forth, sending the pressure of her weight from her heels to her soles to the balls of her feet. She stepped into first position, touching her heels together, her toes facing outward. She squatted down and rose back up, then stepped into second. Down, up, third.

Emma began to dance. Freely at first, but the movements had started to seem familiar, until she realized she was performing a routine. It wasn't the same number she had performed that night. In fact, it was one of the first routines she'd ever learned, though it hadn't always been so easy. She must have been seven or eight when she first perfected it, but perfection had been her biggest downfall. Always when it was perfect, always when it had started to come easily, that's when she would fail. That's when she would lose her concentration, would forget to focus.

But now it was as natural as walking. The alley smelled, and there were puddles of god-knows-what everywhere, but she didn't care. When the dance overtook her like it was doing now, like it'd done the day Henry played Pachelbel's *Canon in*

112

D, there was nothing she could do to resist. There was no part of her that wanted it to end.

After some time, Emma heard voices from across the alley, interrupting her quiet moment. They were harder to decipher than the sounds from her earlier eavesdropping, though these voices were louder, less hushed, as they came in closer. When the blurry figures came clearer into view, Emma froze.

Black hair on a tall, gangly body. A carrot top, short and squatty. A posh girl, a blonde, and a few others. Academians, mostly, but also a few...*non-Academians*. Who were these people?

The posh girl (why couldn't Emma remember her name?) slurred her words. "So I guess your *friend* never showed up, Emm-a-*lem*." Her posse trailed behind her.

The smell of liquor on the girl's breath was overwhelming. Was it Bourbon? Whiskey? Emma had been around plenty of liquor before, to her mother's dismay, but she couldn't quite tell what it was. "What are you doing here?" she asked.

"What am *I* doing here?" The girl nearly fell forward, clutching her stomach as she laughed. Tall-guy came to her rescue. He grabbed her by the arm and hoisted her up. "What the hell are *you* doing here?" she said.

"I just...came to be alone." Emma looked at their faces, their eyes unfocused, their bodies wobbly beneath them, and she started to back away. "You're all wasted. Or—" She paused before saying, "I think you should leave."

"Oh, you think so, do you? Well, you wanna know what *I* think?"

The chubby guy, his hair brighter than the sun, spoke softly. "Jane…" He motioned to the posh girl. Right, that was her name—Jane. "She's right," he said. "Let's just go. This alley reeks."

Emma noticed his fingers trembling. He looked past his shoulder with a sense of urgency.

Then the blonde girl fell to her knees and stared up at the sky, her mouth opened wide, the rest of her expression blank. The others in the group sunk to the pavement next to her, dazed. Totally out of it.

What the hell?

Emma looked back at Jane and watched as she pushed carrot-top out of her way and walked toward her again, tall-guy clinging to her side. Was he holding her up or leaning against her? He seemed the sensible one, but his face looked loopier than hers.

"I really think you should go," Emma said.

Jane inched even closer until Emma's back slammed hard against the Dumpster behind her. They were nearly nose-to-nose as the girl reached for her hair and twirled it around her fingers. Her voice a rasp whisper, the girl said, "We've heard

114

enough of what *you* think, Miss Emma. Miss…Overrated. Miss Liar. Miss *I think I'm better than everyone else*." With her other hand, she pressed her palm to Emma's neck, her fingers hard against her skin.

"Let go of me," Emma said.

Jane smiled. "Oh, I don't think so."

"*Do it*, Jane," tall-guy said.

The blonde girl shouted from across the alley. "Yeah, Jane! Come on! *Do it*."

Emma's eyes bore into Jane's. "Do *what?*"

Just then, Emma heard a softer voice. Distant. "Emma?" it called.

Jane glared at tall-guy. "Who was that?"

The voice grew louder. "Emma?"

All four of them—Emma, Jane, and the two boys—turned to look at the source.

"Emma!" she heard again, a shout that echoed across the alley.

She could barely tell it was him from the other side of the alley, and with Jane and the two boys blocking her view, but of course it was him. Who else would it be? Hardly used to shouting, she allowed her voice to build in her lungs first. Then the scream bellowed out of her.

"Henry!"

Just as he started to run toward her, Jane's fingers pressed deeper into the skin on her neck, digging right on her pressure points. Emma's chest tightened as she struggled for air. She felt her blood, hot and thick, as it rushed to her face.

Henry arrived in seconds. He grabbed Jane by the collar of her jacket and flung her away, and Emma heard the girl's back slam against the wall, then her head, and she fell to the ground. Blonde-girl, breaking further out of her daze, scurried up to comfort Jane.

As Emma let out her breath, coughing for air, tall-guy's face grew red with anger. He locked his eyes on Henry as he stumbled toward him, the orange-haired guy following closely behind.

"Let's just get out of here," Emma said, reaching her hand for Henry's, but he swatted her away. His gaze was fixed. "Henry, these guys are stoned…or something. Please, let's just go. It isn't worth it."

Emma stood there and watched as he ignored her request. He faced the two guys in front of him while she stepped aside, cradling her neck with her hands.

A million scenarios ran through her mind: Henry, hot with anger, lunging into a full-on attack on these kids, knocking them unconscious. Or, less likely, the two of them being stronger than Henry—with strength in numbers and perhaps the drugs that swam through their bloodstreams—beating the shit out of Henry. The repercussions that would follow. The police…the Academy…*her parents*…

She hoped he could hear the warning, if not the desperation, in her voice. "Henry, *please!*"

"Get out of here, Emma," he snapped back. He rolled up his sleeves revealing skinny, scrawny arms, and when she didn't respond or start to run, he turned his face toward her. "I said go! *Now.*"

She crossed her arms over her chest. "No, I'm not leaving. Not without you."

The two boys still had eyes locked on Henry as they made their way slowly toward him. Emma could see more clearly the others from the group as they shuffled around, making their way to their feet. The group began to assemble behind the boys, and even with their eyes glazed over and their limbs wobbly, fear rose up in her chest.

There were six of them. *Six.* Four of them boys.

She tried again. "Please, can we just go!"

She watched as Henry reached into his pocket and pulled out a blade, tiny and smooth. He turned to face her, his skin beet-red. Beads of sweat trickled down his face.

"Get out of here Emma, or I swear to God, it'll be you first." He reached for her bag and threw it toward her.

So this is it, she thought. *Him or me.* And even though she knew he was bluffing, she knew there was no way to stop him either, so she grabbed her bag and ran. At the far end of the alley, she stopped and turned to look at the group. She was far enough away that she could barely make out what was happening, but she could tell the brawl had ensued. She reached for her phone and called the police.

It wasn't long before she could hear the sirens winding in the distance. It seemed the group could hear the sirens too, and as soon as they did they ran from the alley, leaving Henry splayed-out on the ground. She walked up to him, a sight to be seen. His face lay in a pool of blood, and chunks of gravel stuck to his skin. His eyes opened wide as Emma approached.

"You're hurt," she said. She reached for the collar of his shirt and hoisted him up to his feet.

His head bobbed from side to side as he tried to focus. "It's not too bad."

"And the others?"

"They're fine. Stoned out of their minds, but OK."

She examined his face. "Yet they managed to do such damage."

Henry stood up taller and brushed the gravel from his chest. "It wasn't that bad."

She nodded. "Well, the police are on their way."

"Good," he said.

After several moments she spoke again, letting her anger

show in her voice. She was choking back tears. "No, Henry. It's not good!" Her skin flushed red, and before she knew it, her hand had burned across the side of his face.

Henry reached for his cheek. "What the hell was that for?"

"Because of how stupid you are! Why did you have to go and do that? I was just fine!"

"You were *not* fine. Those guys had you cornered. They were out of their minds. And they had a purpose, Emma. Didn't you see the look on Jane's face? She wanted to *kill* you."

"Maybe so. But did you really think it better that they kill us both?"

"They didn't! Look at us, we're OK. And now the police are almost here."

"Yes, exactly," she said. "The police are almost here. And do you know what that means? It means you'll get kicked out of Academy. You can't have violence on your record. You can't—"

Henry stopped her with a lowered voice, his hands held out toward her. "I was just trying to protect you."

"I am not *yours* to protect, OK? When will you understand that?"

"You really want to make this about *that*? You know I would've fought back for anyone. You know *anyone* would've fought back for you. But since you decided to bring all this up, tell me Emma, why aren't you mine to protect? Why the hell not?"

"You know why. For the hundredth time, I don't have time—"

"Don't give me that shit," he said. "Is it because of who I am? Is that it? You're embarrassed of me?"

She shook her head. "We've gone over this once before…"

"Yeah, well, maybe I don't believe what was said before. I don't see any other reason for you to treat me like you do. Not *ever*. And especially not tonight."

As the police finally turned the corner, Emma stopped to consider his question. Before the cops rolled to a stop and consumed them both with questioning, she turned to Henry and said, "Yes, that's it. That's the reason I can't be with you."

And she allowed him to believe it was true, no matter that it was a lie.

• • •

Chloe knocked back the last sip of her coffee and slid the empty mug to the end of the table, exchanging it for Emma's which sat untouched, still full to the brim.

"I remember that," Chloe said. "I mean, I remember everyone getting kicked out afterward. Jane and those two guys. The whole thing was kind of hush-hush though. I had no idea it happened like *that*."

"I was so sure they'd kick out Henry. Being, you know…Henry."

"Right. He wasn't exactly Academy's favorite."

"Right."

"So what happened next?"

"Well, that's the thing," Emma told her. "After our big fight, it all gets kind of fuzzy. I wasn't even certain they kicked out the others until you just told me."

"Really? Fuzzy?"

"I don't know how else to explain it. It's like, I *know* what happened, but I don't really *remember* it happening."

Chloe nodded. "Like 9/11?"

"Sort of, but not exactly. That whole day is just kind of…blank. Sometimes I'll see in my mind a quick flash of a scene, but I can't tell if I dreamed it up or not. I can't tell if I'm just remembering nightmares."

Chloe's face grew sullen but she continued, determined to figure all of this out. "9/11 happened, what, two weeks after your fight with Henry?"

"Yeah, just about."

"So you have this vivid memory of fighting with Henry, and then for two weeks everything is kind of fuzzy. Then September 11th rolls around and…*nothing*?"

Emma nodded. "Yes, nothing."

"What's the next thing you remember?"

She thought for a moment. "I remember being home, just me and Mom and Lois, and I remember knowing what had happened, that my father had died. And I realized, then, that I didn't actually *remember* it. There were no memories that were just *mine*. Only the ones I'd been handed, the things people told me."

"Do you remember the moment you found out?"

She shook her head. "No. I don't remember finding out, not the exact moment of it. I just remember it being later—a day later, a week later, I don't know—and by then I just sort of knew."

"So, OK," Chloe began, "tell me what you remember from those two weeks."

"Even though it's fuzzy?"

Chloe nodded.

"Well, the next day, after our big fight, rumors on campus are already beginning to swirl. That Henry had *killed* someone. That *he* had been killed. That it was all because of me. And I know what everyone is thinking. *What's so special about Emma, anyway?* So the other students glare at me, but I let it roll right off. I keep to myself, as always, but the whole time my emotions are stewing inside me, and I can't quite put my finger on what it is I'm feeling. Anger? Sadness? Longing... One thing is for certain: Henry won't be coming back to Academy. Not even if he wants to. And most likely, I think, he wants to. But the standards at Academy are high, and the rules are strict, especially when it comes to students instigating fights. And that's what had happened, wasn't it? According to Academy? *He* was the instigator, and hadn't he known the school would punish him for fighting?"

"Of course they would," Chloe added. "Even if it was to protect the girl he was in love with."

"Yeah," Emma said, "and so I start to wonder, is Henry really *in love* with me? Is it true what he said, that those guys had wanted to kill me? And would *anyone* have really intervened?"

She reached for her coffee and sipped it slowly before continuing. "By the end of the week, I can't stand it any longer. I need answers. I need to know if he's all right. But mostly, what I need from Henry is *closure*. So when the school bell rings at 3:45 on Friday afternoon, I hail a cab and head straight to the Upper West Side, to Henry's house."

"OK," Chloe acknowledged.

"I remember the quiet street he lived on, the large brownstone, the row of multi-colored façades. I adored his neighborhood, spotless and beautiful yet so much less pretentious than my own.

"I look up at his home from the window of the cab and,

after a few steady breaths, I tip the driver and get out, then I make my way up the big concrete steps. Before I can manage to knock, I stand in frozen silence, staring at the heavy doors in front of me, wondering what I'll even say. *What will Henry say?* When I feel like I've composed myself enough, I knock. Three even, steady knocks. Henry's niece answers. You know Tabitha. Blonde pigtails and pale skin, rosy cheeks, bright blue eyes. As she opens the door, she places her hand on her hip, all sass. She's probably not even three years old yet."

Chloe smiled. By now she must have known Tabitha as well as Emma had back then. Probably more so. "What did she say?" Chloe asked.

"She says, '*You* haven't been around to visit much. Why not?' She opens her big blue eyes wide and pouts her lips. I crouch down to my knees and say, 'I'm sorry, Tabby. I've been busy.' Then I reach out my hands and run my fingers through her pigtails. 'Is your uncle around?' I ask. 'Yeah,' she says. 'He's upstairs.' And then she adds, 'I think he's still packing.'"

"Packing?" Chloe asked.

"Right! You can imagine my surprise. So I ask just that. '*Packing?*' And Tabby says, 'Yeah. Because he's moving back to Albuquerque. Isn't that why you're here? To say goodbye?'

"The news hits me like a storm, but I maintain my composure. 'Y—yeah,' I manage. 'That's why I came. To say goodbye. Can you get him for me, please?' Tabby nods. 'All right!' she chirps, and closes the door behind her before fluttering up the stairs."

Chloe held up a finger, pausing Emma. "Wait, she fluttered up the stairs?"

"Yeah, why?"

"How do you know she fluttered up the stairs if you were still standing alone on the porch?"

"Um…" Emma hesitated. "I don't know, exactly. I guess I just assumed. Maybe I could hear her?"

"Maybe." Chloe shook her head. "Anyways, continue."

"While I'm waiting, I pace around the front porch, thinking of the last time I'd seen Henry. It was the last time I'd heard from him too. I'm thinking: *Why hasn't he called me since then? Why hasn't he told me he's leaving?* Those questions start to fester inside me, and it makes me so angry. By the time Henry opens the door, I'm like…*raging* mad."

Chloe nodded. "Right, yeah. So then what?"

"Well, Henry finally comes out. He steps onto the porch and closes the door behind him. He looks at me, his face apologetic, mine hot with anger, and for a while neither of us speaks. Until finally, Henry begins. 'You're probably expecting an explanation,' he says. I just stand there, quiet, waiting. He goes on. 'First, I'm sorry.' 'Oh?' I say. 'You're *sorry*? Why, what in the world would you have to be sorry for? For not calling me? For ignoring me all week? I mean, what were you gonna do, Henry? Just leave without ever telling me? Without ever talking to me again?' And he says, 'No...I was going to tell you. Really I was. I just...didn't know how. Or if—'

"I give him a condescending pat on the shoulder. 'Oh, I know how hard it would have been for you. To pick up the phone and say, *Hey Emma. By the way, I'm leaving. So I guess I'll never see you again. But...whatever. Bye!*'"

"What does he say to that?" Chloe asked.

"Well, nothing at first. He reaches out to me, wraps his arms around me and pulls me close to him. I resist him, but I know there's no getting out from his hold, so I relax my head against his chest. Then he says, 'For the hundredth time, Emma. I'm sorry.' 'Actually,' I tell him, 'you only said it twice.' To this, Henry smiles and says, 'Well, I really am.'"

Emma noticed Chloe leaning far over the table, like she was really interested, but she couldn't tell if Chloe believed what she was saying or not. "So you made up?" Chloe asked.

"Not exactly. We stand together, embracing each other like that for a few quiet moments, and my emotions have all but calmed before they blow up again."

"Blow up?"

"Yeah. I push my hand against his chest and my eyes fill up with tears. 'I can never forgive you,' I tell him. 'I can never forgive you for getting kicked out of Academy…for leaving me.' And he says, 'Kicked out of Academy? I didn't get kicked out.' For a moment my crying stops. '*What?*' I ask, and then he says, and here's the real kicker: 'I withdrew.' My mouth drops open. 'What?' I say. 'Why would you—' He interrupts me. 'Emma, listen to me. It's for the best. You don't need me getting in your way anymore. You don't need me holding you back. Besides, there's nothing for me here. I'll do so much better in Albuquerque. It's more…*me*, you know?'"

"What did he mean by that?" Chloe asked.

"I have no idea. I look away from him and say nothing as I consider what he's told me. When I turn back to face him, my skin is still burning with anger, my cheeks red from crying. My lip trembles, my eyes search his. Then, unthinkingly, my hand flies across the side of his face."

Chloe gasped. "You hit him *again?*"

"Oh, it gets worse," Emma said. "I start screaming at him. 'I hate you!' I say. 'I hate you, Henry! I hate you!' And I continue to hit him, my hands balling up against him, but he catches my fists mid-air. 'If you hate me so much,' he says, 'you should be happy I'm leaving.' His eyes are looking deep into mine as he speaks, his voice firm. 'Well, I'm *not* happy you're leaving,' I tell him. 'I'm furious!' 'Why?' he asks. 'Give me one good reason why.' And I say, 'Because I care about you, Henry! I care about you! That's why I didn't want you protecting me, because I didn't want to lose you.' And then…"

Chloe's eyes were wide open as she listened. "And then *what?*"

"Then I tell him that I love him. And that I don't want him to leave."

"And did he—"

"Say it back?" Emma looked down at her now half-full coffee. "Not exactly. He puts his hands on my shoulders and pulls me against him again, and then all of a sudden his hands are on the sides of my face, and his lips press against mine. I allow it to happen. My mouth melts against the heat of his kiss, and my whole body grows weak.

"When Henry finally releases me, his eyes are searching my face. 'So the truth comes out,' he says. And I say, 'Don't leave me, Henry. Say you'll stay here with me.'"

"Oh," Chloe said. "So he agreed to stay? For you?"

"No, he went back to Albuquerque. How did you not hear about that?"

"I'm not sure, Emma." Chloe's face twisted in contemplation. "It's not making sense. How did you end things with him, *exactly?*"

"Well, after I ask him to stay, he shakes his head. He says, 'I meant what I said before—about you, about your dreams. I'm no good for you, Emma. I'm nowhere near good enough for you. And you…you were right all along. I see that now. You have bigger dreams than just me.'"

Chloe let out a heavy breath. "Wow," she said.

"Wow is right! I felt so vulnerable, so heartbroken, defeated… Before I'd gone to see Henry that day, I thought I'd lost my best friend. I thought I'd been given the cold shoulder, been ignored by Henry out of pity or spite. But now I felt so much more. Now I knew how I really felt about Henry. Now Henry knew too. Everything inside me had been spilled out in those few moments, yet I'd be the one alone, abandoned, left behind. I didn't want Henry stopping me from reaching my dreams, and now… God. Now I couldn't have let him stop me if I tried."

"Did you try again after that?"

"No," Emma said. "I knew Henry would leave. He was decided. Shit, he was *packed*. He had dreams of his own now, and I knew I had already said enough. So…still standing close to Henry, I push my hand against his chest again, then I back far away from him and nod my farewell. I don't say anything as I turn around and walk away. I don't stop. I don't even look back."

"And it was just one week later that—"

"Yeah, Chloe. Just one week, and I'd lose everything."

Chloe nodded. "And now three years later, here you are."

"Yep, back in the City. Back to dancing. And somehow, it

seems, I'm back to Henry."

CHAPTER 9

They sat in silence while the waitress filled up their mugs, hearing little more than the dishes clink and the muddled conversations in the diner. The wind had started to pick up outside.

Finally, Chloe spoke. "I had no idea."

Emma shrugged. "Well, now you know."

"I should have been there. I should have seen your performance."

"What do you mean? Your introduction wasn't until the following week."

"I should have been there for *you*. For moral support, you know? God, some friend I was."

"I didn't go to yours."

"Right…" Chloe's voice broke off and a heavy silence fell between them again. Then she continued, "So that was that?"

"Yeah," Emma said. "I never heard from him again. I haven't seen him since."

"Until tonight."

"Right."

"But you wanted to."

"What?" Emma furrowed her brows and brought the coffee mug up to her lips. "*No.*"

Chloe sat still, seemingly mulling it over. "So you tell

someone you love them, and then you're perfectly fine with never seeing them again?"

"It wasn't like that."

"Wasn't like what?"

"It wasn't that simple."

"What was so complicated?"

"His being gone…it made me hate him. *Really* hate him."

"He left for *you*, Emma. You said it yourself."

Emma darted her eyes away from Chloe, but Chloe reached her hand across the table, her fingers soft as she placed them over Emma's wrist.

"It's like that thing, you know? If you love someone, you let them go."

Emma turned her gaze back to Chloe. "I didn't hate him for leaving. I hated him for not coming back. And if he didn't want to come back, then I didn't want him to either."

"Had you ever asked him to come back?"

"He should have known! He knew I loved him by then. And he knew what had happened. He knew my father worked in those towers. And my mother…" She turned her face away from Chloe. "If he really left for me, he would have come back for me too."

"Maybe he tried."

"Yeah, maybe," she said disbelievingly, wishing their talk

could be over already.

Chloe sipped her coffee slowly. "You never did tell me what happened with your mother. How you and Lois ended up in Oregon."

Emma feigned a smile. "Another day. One thing at a time."

"Fair enough. Shall we head back home then?"

"Sure, and it'll be your turn to tell me what you've been up to for the past three years."

Chloe nodded. She reached into her handbag and placed a twenty on the table. "Emma, can I just say one more thing?"

"Yeah," Emma said. "Sure."

"You lost your dad, I know. And then somehow you lost your mom too. Then you lost the will to dance, but you got it back, and you came home—"

"And my home—"

"I know, Emma. I *know*. You lost everything. And some of those things you won't get back so easily, or…ever. But you never lost Henry. And you'll *never* lose me."

"I did lose—"

Chloe shook her head. Her eyes brightened. "No, Emma. No you didn't."

Emma swallowed hard. "But he never even called."

"You wouldn't have answered."

"I would have at least liked the chance not to." She felt the ridiculousness of the words on her lips, but she still couldn't *not* say them.

Chloe let out her breath, exasperated. "Emma, do you know he comes to the City, like, every chance he gets?"

"Yeah, so?"

"Do you know he plays at that bar every time he's here?"

"You told me already."

"And do you know he comes right up to me afterward? That he doesn't ever talk to anyone else?"

Emma rolled her eyes. "Maybe *you* should date him then."

Chloe's mouth tightened into a thin line. "That'd be like dating my brother."

"Your brother? You guys weren't even friends in high school."

"Well, we're friends now. One of the many things that have changed around here. So get used to it, OK? And while you're getting used to things, you should get used to the fact that Henry is still in love with you."

In love with her? After all this time? Emma's heart began to race. "*What?*" she said, louder than she intended.

"Yeah, and he asks about you every time he's here. Not that I've had any answers for him. You haven't exactly kept in touch with me either."

Emma stood from the table, her tone defensive. "Do you even have a point?"

Patiently, Chloe reached for Emma's hand and guided her back into the booth. Her voice was calm.

"Emma, Henry had a pretty damn good reason for not calling you, just trust me on that. But he came back to the City as soon as he could. He came back for *you*. He *keeps* coming back for you."

This was news to Emma, though to be honest she wasn't surprised. Henry had loved her before. A selfless, undeserving kind of love that had overwhelmed her. It was a love she knew she'd never be able to reciprocate. In spite of the way she felt about him in return, it wouldn't have been enough. He would have disagreed if she'd said it to him, but Emma knew the truth: that Henry Hayes was just too damn good for her.

The two girls sat quietly again. Their waitress passed by the table, picked up the cash and closed the tab. The tables around them had all cleared out and the music became too low to hear.

Emma turned to Chloe again, this time with a change of subject. "I have Juilliard auditions in just a few months."

"Yeah?"

"I'll need shoes, a leotard, everything I lost in the fire. My purse, even." She hoped Chloe would take the hint. With just one call to Augusta, she knew there'd be money on the way to repay her.

"OK," Chloe said.

"And I'll need a place to practice. Your apartment probably

won't work."

Chloe smiled brightly and stood up from the booth. She reached her hand out to Emma. "Well," she said, "I'm so glad you asked."

The walk seemed longer because of the chill. It was barely autumn, but at nearly three o'clock in the morning the air was crisp. A strong wind whipped around the City, leaves fluttering out of the trees and strewn across the sidewalks. Chloe and Emma walked close together until they arrived at Chloe's secret destination.

It was tucked away in the East Village on the second floor of a corner building, right above a pizza joint. Chloe took Emma's hand and led her up the stairs. She dug through her purse for keys.

"What is this place?"

"You'll see," Chloe said, still digging around. Then she swung the door open and flicked on the lights, revealing a single room with four white walls and hardwood floors. A mirror spanned the length of the far wall. A ballet barre stretched from wall to wall in front of it.

Emma's jaw dropped open. "No way! You have your own studio?"

"Well, not my *own*." Chloe gave a humble grin. "I have a partner, but she doesn't know much about dance. She makes the executive decisions, for the most part, and I just take care of the dancing."

"Take care of?"

"Yeah, I teach."

Emma walked up to the mirrored wall and ran her fingers along the barre. "Second best thing to Juilliard, huh?"

"Emma…" Chloe hesitated.

"Yeah?"

"I wasn't denied by Juilliard."

"Oh, you weren't? Then why—"

"Like I said, a lot's changed around here. After…*everything*…I wanted to do something good. I didn't want to be stuck in school for two years, or four, or more. And to be honest with you, I didn't want to be *just* another dancer." Emma watched as Chloe considered her curious expression. "Not that there's anything wrong with that." It seemed they were both equally embarrassed.

"So you opened a studio," Emma said. "And now you teach."

"Yeah." Chloe smiled. "For free."

"For *what?*"

"It's more of a mentoring program, Em. A non-profit. Dancing is just the icing on the cake."

"Sort of like the Boys and Girls Club, or the Y?"

"Yeah," Chloe said. "Something like that."

Emma pondered this as she looked around the room, what couldn't have been bigger than Chloe's living room. But this was Manhattan, and the East Village at that. She knew it must have cost a fortune.

"Must be some business partner you have."

"Actually, yeah." Chloe walked closer to Emma, her eyes smiling. "It's Ms. Hayes, Henry's mom. And all of this?" Reading the surprise on Emma's face, she spread out her arms and turned full-circle in the center of the room. "It was all her idea."

"That's…quite the surprise. I had no idea you two—"

"They're good people, Emma. And they've missed you. We all have."

Emma stood still, quiet, managing a small smile. She allowed Chloe's hand to slip once more into hers.

"You can practice here if you'd like," Chloe said. "We're closed on Sundays, but I'll give you the key."

"Is it already Sunday?" Emma asked, and Chloe simply nodded. "Yeah, I guess I'll come by first thing in the morning. Oh, except—"

"Right. Shopping first."

CHAPTER 10

If he hadn't chickened out, Henry would've seen the skeletal remains of Emma's house that same night, right after he finished his set at the bar, but instead he decided to wait. She obviously hadn't wanted to see him. Not there, unexpectedly, so soon after she returned. Hadn't she made it clear? The look on her face. The way she left in such a hurry.

Now, Emma was a lot of things, but hard to read she was not. She always made herself clear to Henry. At least, that's what he told himself that night.

So he'd wake up early the next morning, wash down half a protein bar with an energy drink, stretch and do push-ups hours before his mom and niece would even begin to stir. Then he'd go for his routine homecoming jog through Central Park. It'd be full of Sunday runners and weekend tourists kicking up autumn leaves as they went. The wind would steadily blow. A heavy layer of dew would blanket the grass. And just before he'd finish, the sun would rise up, burnt orange against the buildings, and the birds would start to sing.

Damn, what a view.

It usually took just an hour for Henry to run the perimeter of the park, but after forty-five minutes he barely made it halfway around, slowed down by thoughts of Emma, running on hardly any sleep. Had he really been so surprised to see her?

He wanted to bump into her in the City again. He hoped she'd show up at the bar one night; he counted on Chloe to bring her there. But it didn't make sense to happen this weekend. The timing…well, it sucked.

An hour into the run, Henry finds himself on Emma's street, three short blocks from her house, or what he assumes is still her house because nobody new has ever moved in. The curtains in the window have always remained. A ceramic flowerpot has stood for years, unmoved in the entryway.

Not that he passed by routinely, or anything.

As Henry turns toward her house, his pace slows to a steady walk, and he starts to wonder: what would he say if he saw her running on the opposite side of the street? Would he say hello, manage to strike up a conversation, or would he pretend not to notice, keep his head down, turn the music up loud on his iPod? And Emma, how would she react to seeing him…again?

But as it turns out, he has nothing to worry about.

Henry stands on the steps of Emma's old Upper East Side home sectioned off with caution tape. He looks up at the ravaged façade and he can tell from his training that it burned little more than a day ago. He knows about her father, and Chloe had once suggested something about her mother, too, but she doesn't seem to know a whole lot more than he does.

140

He knows Emma moved to Oregon with her sister (did their mother go with them?), and he'd gotten a heads-up from Chloe—a little too late—about her returning. But he doesn't know how bad it's all been. He doesn't know how hard it's been for Emma to come back here. Did she set the house on fire herself? Was her childhood home so full of haunting memories that it had to be destroyed? He can't imagine how that can be true. They were a perfect loving family, struck with tragedy, but he always assumed the girls would recover. Emma and Lois would recover from this. And Emma, she'd never do something so reckless. But then again, Emma has always been full of surprises.

As he stands here gawking, the front door opens and a group of official-looking men exit the house. Police, investigators. Insurance guys, probably. They make their way down the steps, and one of them looks at Henry. "Hey, you live here?"

"No sir, I—"

"Then keep it movin', aight? Nothin' to see here." Henry notices the small crowd of people that have started to gather in the street behind him. "Come on folks, keep it movin'!"

He nods, half-dazed, and takes a small step back. After the men have already passed by him and gotten into their cars, Henry runs toward them. "Wait!" He taps politely on the glass, and one of the officers—insurance guy, whatever he is—does not look pleased.

Henry manages to catch his breath. "The girl...Emma Jenkins?"

"You know Miss Jenkins?"

He nods.

The officer smiles. "She's all right, son."

Henry grows eager. "You know where she's staying?"

"I'm afraid I'm not at liberty to—"

"But she's in the Village, right? Can you just tell me if she's staying in the Village?"

The officer smirks. "I don't know why you even asked, if—
"

"Was it arson, sir? I mean, officer...sir?" He can hardly swallow the emotions that have knotted up in the back of his throat.

The officer reaches out the window and pats Henry on the shoulder. "It was an accident, son. These things happen."

Henry breathes a sigh of relief and begins to turn away from him.

"Hey!" The officer cruises up to him. "Since you're so friendly with Miss Jenkins, you may tell her that we're done here. Let her know the scene has been released."

"The what?"

"The scene." He points back to the house. "Her home? Tell

her she can come look through it. See what's left to salvage."

"You mean, she can get her stuff?"

"Right, just have her call ahead, OK?"

"Yeah, sure," Henry says. "Thanks."

As the man drives off, Henry reaches into the pocket of his sweatpants and pulls out his cell phone. He shoots a text to Chloe.

Passed by house. Scene released.

He presses send, then types another.

Little heads-up woulda been nice.

He puts the phone back in his pocket, turns up the volume on his iPod, and heads for his home just on the other side of the park, but before he's even gotten to the end of the street Henry stops dead in his tracks. He turns around slowly, facing back toward Emma's home, considering. The officer's words echo.

See what's left to salvage.

He shakes his head and whispers to himself. It's still private property. *Emma's* private property. It'd be wrong, not to mention illegal. It would be totally crossing the line.

Then, the next thing he knows, Henry is standing by the steps again, in front of the caution tape, looking up at the broken façade.

• • •

Emma was sitting at the edge of her seat in the corner of the store, her fourth attempt at a new pair of dance shoes, when Chloe's phone vibrated.

She motioned to Emma before stepping outside to answer it.

"Hello?"

His breathing was particularly heavy. "Hey, did you get my message?"

"No. What message?"

"I was out for a run, and I passed by Emma's."

"Oh, right. How was it?"

"Really bad, Chlo. Why didn't you tell me?"

"I'm sorry, but I haven't exactly had time, what with Emma crashing on my couch, then our little rendezvous at your bar, and we all know how that turned out…"

"Yeah, I was gonna ask you about that."

"Now is not the best time," she said. "I'm at the store with Emma. She needs…well, you know. Everything."

"Sounds like a blast. I'm guessing you'll be there all day."

"Most definitely."

"Well, when you're done, tell Emma the cops have turned the house over to her. She just has to call, then she can go take a look at her things. See if there's anything, you know, *worthy of*

144

keeping."

Emma appeared in the window holding a shoebox in her hand. She opened the door with the other. "Chloe, who are you talking to?"

Chloe snapped her cell phone shut. "The fire department. They're done looking at your home. You can go get your stuff."

"The fire department? How'd they know to call you?"

She hesitated. "They, uh…they didn't. My mom called them. To…check on things."

"And then they called *you?*"

"Right," Chloe said. "Yeah."

Emma's face grew more suspicious, but the expression quickly cleared away. "Well, that's OK." She swiped at the air with an open hand. "I don't need to go."

"What? Emma, you need to go back. You need to look through your stuff. Some of it may be salvageable."

She shook her head. "I don't think so."

"Emma…"

"I said I'm not going back, OK? It's time for me to start over."

"I don't think—"

"Look, Chloe, I know. It sucks what happened, but I can't keep dwelling on things. I have to just take it as a sign. Start over. All new stuff." She motioned to the box in her hand and lifted the lid. "Like these shoes. What do you think?"

"Yeah, they're nice," Chloe said. They really were.

"Aren't they? I can't wait to try them out."

Chloe forced her sincerest smile as she reached into her pocket, pulling out a set of keys. She slipped one off and handed it to Emma. "Well, like I said, it's all yours. You can stay as long as you like." She led her to the cash register and, in the brief moment that Emma stood with her back to her, Chloe reached for her phone again.

Emma not going back. Studio instead.

She pressed send, then sent another: *Looks like it's your turn.*

• • •

The apartment percolates with the smell of breakfast. Not just any breakfast: Mom's breakfast. Homemade biscuits and flour gravy, fried potatoes, sausage and eggs cooked so perfectly over-easy that only the most experienced of chefs could replicate them.

Henry's mom stands in the kitchen, in front of the stove, her bathrobe tied snugly around her. She stirs the gravy, relentlessly but slow. Her face is nearly drained of color. "Henry James Hayes! Please tell me you did not go inside that girl's house."

"Shhh, Tabitha's still asleep." Henry reaches inside the cabinets for a large porcelain dish, then spoons the potatoes into it. "Anyway, there's nothing to worry about. I didn't do it. Not yet at least."

"Not *yet?* Henry, why would you even think—"

"Chloe said she won't go back. Like she's just gonna leave all her stuff there to be auctioned off or destroyed or, I don't know, whatever they do after a fire in the City."

"Well, isn't that Emma's choice to make, whether or not she goes back for her stuff? Maybe she doesn't think there's anything worth saving. And she would know, right? What with it being *her house* and all."

"No, Ma. She's not thinking straight."

"And you're to judge when Emma Jenkins is not thinking straight? You hardly knew her before you left."

"I knew her well enough." He sets the potatoes aside and takes a long, slow sip from a cup of coffee, then he slams the mug down on the counter. "I *still* know her."

His mother isn't fazed. "I don't think you do, Henry. And I don't think she knows you that well either. A lot's happened in the last few years."

"Yeah, a lot's happened, and I wasn't here for it. I *left*, right when she really needed me. More than ever. And now she *hates* me."

She tightens the robe around her waist. "There was no way

you could have known everything that would come of it, all that would happen with Emma, with her family. You thought you were doing the best thing by her, remember? It's a *good thing*, what you've done. And to think that Emma hates you now is just ridiculous."

"You didn't see the look on her face."

"No, I didn't, but I can imagine. She was surprised—shocked, even, to see you. But did you ever stop and wonder why, exactly? Did you ever think that maybe Emma thinks *you* hate *her*?"

"Now *that* is ridiculous. I left *for her*, I was really clear about that. She knows I could never have hated her. She knows I *loved* her."

His mom shrugs. "Love, hate. Tomayto, tomahto." She hands Henry the spatula and nods him toward the gravy to stir, then she kisses him on the cheek. "Just don't do anything stupid, Henry."

CHAPTER 11

Emma had been practicing in Chloe's studio for nearly eight hours when she heard what sounded like a faint tap at the door. She stopped abruptly and looked at the clock. It was nearly midnight.

Tap tap tap.

She furrowed her brows. *What the hell was that?* On dainty feet, she tip-toed to the stereo and turned down the music.

Tap tap. Tap tap.

Someone at the door. Chloe? Emma made her way over and slipped the lock aside, huffily. "I know it's getting late, Chlo, but you didn't have to come all the way—" She opened the door, and her stomach dropped. She sucked in her breath. "Oh," she said as chocolate-brown eyes smiled back at her from across the threshold.

He leaned his side against the frame. "Sorry," he said. "You expected someone prettier."

It took a moment before she could speak. What was there to say? "What are you doing here, Henry?" It was the best she could do.

"Chloe said you'd be here."

Chloe! And she couldn't have called with a teeny, tiny warning? *Hey Emma, sweet friend, just so you know…that guy you kissed three years ago, the one you said 'I love you' to and haven't seen since, remember him? Well, he's on his way. Like,* now.

And of course, it had to be while Emma was wearing little more than a leotard, dripping with sweat, breathless from dancing. And she was definitely breathless now.

From dancing. Right.

"Can I come in please?"

Emma nodded and stepped aside. "Yeah, sure."

"Thanks," he said. She closed the door gently behind him.

Henry walked halfway around the room, then up to the mirror. He ran his fingers along the ballet barre. All the while Emma stood still by the door, her heart like a hammer in her chest, pounding hard. "So why'd you come here, Henry?" she asked again.

He leaned forward against the barre, and his eyes met hers through their reflections in the mirror. "I thought it'd only be fair. You got to watch me perform, so now it's my turn."

"That was entirely different," Emma said curtly. "I'm *practicing*, not performing."

"I suspected you'd say that. Which leads me to Plan B." He turned around and grinned, then made his way to her from across the room.

Her body tightened, her face flushed with heat as Henry came closer, until they were standing face-to-face. "Plan B?"

"Dinner." He smiled cheekily.

Emma gazed at Henry, his face so close to hers, noticing again all the little ways he'd changed. His features had hardened; his skin looked rough and tan. His chest and shoulders were bigger, *stronger*, and he'd grown at least another inch. But he was familiar. A pool of comfort she thought she could drown in. His eyes, his smile, *those lips*. Where was the boy she'd known in high school? What were those familiar features doing on the face of this man in front of her?

She took a deep breath and her eyes flitted away from his. "I'm not hungry."

"Not hungry? Chloe said you've been here for hours. And you haven't eaten all day."

"Right." Emma nodded. "*Chloe said*."

He placed his hands in his pockets. "If I didn't know better I'd say you were jealous."

"*Jealous? Of what?*"

"I don't know." He shrugged. "The way some things have changed around here. Like with me and Chloe, being friends and all."

"You think I care that you and Chloe are friends?"

"Emma, I didn't mean—"

"No, Henry. Listen to me. The only thing I wish hadn't changed around here is *your* being here. Or do you not remember running back to Albuquerque for no damn good reason at all?" She looked at him with hard eyes. With her arms crossed over her chest, she stomped across the room and turned up the volume on the stereo.

Henry remained where he was, raising his voice above the music. "What are you doing?"

"Practicing." She placed her hand over the barre and stepped back into position. She glanced at Henry. "You can see yourself out."

Henry nodded and made his way toward the door, and Emma had barely begun her routine before he stopped again. He stood still for a few long moments, his back to her. Then he finally turned around.

"I went by your house this morning," he said, his voice low.

Emma froze. He did *what?*

"Emma?"

She remained still, staring at her feet against the hardwood floor. She wished he hadn't gone to her house. She wished, if he had, that there'd been nothing to see, because everything would have still been perfect. If she hadn't lit the candles; if she hadn't thought she was ready for all of this, hadn't thought she could have actually had that moment of peace; if she hadn't come back in the first place...

Henry walked closer to her. "Emma?" he said again.

Her breath became choked. She said nothing.

He reached out to her, his hand grazing her shoulder, and

just as he'd probably expected she might, Emma jerked away from him. Her face had become moist and reddened, and her lips were trembling, her eyes welled up with tears. But it didn't stop Henry; maybe it had even propelled him forward, because in one swift motion he took her arms with both of his hands and pulled her against him, his arms wrapped firmly around her, holding tightly against his chest, her breaths stuttering loudly now, her sobs thick and heavy.

And then, just like it'd done at Academy so many years ago, the music that played moved them both into rhythm, and they began to sway. Slowly at first, side to side, tangled up in each other's embrace. As the song continued, Henry reached for Emma's hand, soft and warm in his, and spun her slowly around. Her breathing steadied, in and out against his chest.

Then, after some time, Henry placed gentle fingers on the side of her face. He tucked her hair behind her ears. She wondered what he thought of the length of her hair... What a silly thing. But it was back to normal now, the way it had been just the day before he'd met her at Academy. Long and heavy.

"Let me take you home."

"No, I can manage." She inhaled deeply and wiped the tears from her cheeks. "It's only four blocks to Chloe's."

"Yeah, but it's past midnight, and you don't seem—"

"I'm fine, really. And besides, it's a *safe* four blocks."

"Safer with me," he said. He curled her arm through his.

Emma smiled. How many times had they walked together like this? Arms tangled? She relented. "Let me just close things down here first, OK?"

"Yeah," he said. "I'll wait outside."

• • •

It takes Emma longer than just a few minutes to close the studio. Henry wonders what she has to do, and if maybe he should have offered to help. He shakes his head. *No*, he decides, *she needs this time to herself.* He's never seen her so flustered. Oh, who is he kidding, that's a lie; it doesn't take much to fluster this girl. He probably should have called ahead, at least.

No, not that either. She'd never have answered.

So Henry just stands here, waiting as patiently as he possibly can, all things considered, doing his best to steady his nerves before Emma steps out. He starts to pace at the bottom of the stairway. He breathes in the air—crisp, cool, still. He wipes his hands on the sides of his jeans.

Nearly twenty minutes later *(twenty minutes!)*, Emma makes her way down the stairs. Her hair is wet from a shower, all the loose strands pulled back. She's wearing a long yellow skirt that picks up a little with each step she takes. A greenish-blue sweater hangs over her white tank top. She has an oversized bag slung down off one shoulder, and in the opposite hand she holds her ballet shoes.

"Hey." Her tone is quiet but friendly. She smiles. Henry can smell a light misting of perfume as she steps closer—something flowery, maybe, with a hint of citrus.

He reaches for her bag. "I've got that."

"No, that's OK. I can carry it."

"Let me. You look tired from working late."

"Henry, let go. I've got it."

He lets go.

She fixes her hair with her other hand. "I look tired?"

"You look beautiful."

For a full two blocks, Emma and Henry walk without speaking. They stand several paces apart, stealing glances but never catching them (at least, he *thinks* she's doing that too). It isn't until they reach the end of the second block that the fresh-baked smell of cupcakes and just-brewed coffee wafts in front of them, the aroma spilling out of the bakery and onto the sidewalk. Henry reaches for Emma's hand.

"What is this place?"

"Cupcakes," he tells her, smiling proudly. He leads her forward.

She looks at him suspiciously.

"And coffee," he adds.

"At midnight?" Her eyebrows shoot up. She might be smiling too, but who can tell?

"City never sleeps. Don't say you've gone light on me."

"No," she says. "I just never took you for a cupcakes and coffee at midnight kind of guy."

Henry drops her hand as they take their place in the back of the line where just a few people are waiting in front of them. He lowers his voice and says, "I'm whatever kind of guy you don't think I am."

She rolls her eyes. "Oh, mysterious."

"I was going for cryptic."

"That too." She looks up at the menu that hangs overhead. "Hmm, what do I want? What do I want…" Her voice trails off. He wants to tell her he already knows. But he doesn't.

"*Next,*" the guy behind the counter calls.

Henry takes Emma's hand and leads her forward again. "We're ready."

She slips her hand from his. "But I haven't decided—"

"She'll have a small coffee, a French roast if you have, with just one tiny drop of milk. Non-fat. And have it freshly brewed if you can." The cashier punches in the order. "A bottle of water for me, and one vanilla cupcake. No icing." He holds up his fingers. "Two forks."

"Just a few minutes," the guy says nicely. "Take a seat

anywhere."

Henry pays, thanks him, then walks with Emma to a booth in the far corner. They slide into opposite sides.

Emma looks at Henry, her curious expression unchanged. "You hate vanilla cupcakes."

"I don't *hate* them," he tells her. "I just think, you know, there are so many more options. Red velvet, salted caramel, lemon and carrot and...*mystery*." He gives her a wink. A waiter strolls up to their table and hands them each a fork, then slides the coffee toward Emma. A bottle of water for Henry. "Variety is the spice of life," Henry adds.

Emma nearly smiles, but not quite. "Says the guy with the water bottle."

"Right," he says. "Stop folding your lip."

She laughs, then brings the rim of the mug to her mouth and breathes in. "I do love a strong cup of coffee." *Love.* She says the words in the same sharp moment she glances at Henry. Like they still have meaning.

"You know what they say about coffee and water, eh?" Henry lifts up his water bottle and waves it around with too much enthusiasm. A few drops of water spill from the opening and drip into Emma's coffee cup.

"Oh no!"

"Shit! I'll have them make you a new one."

"Mmm, it's good," Emma says. "No, I kind of like it."

They sit and eat in comfortable silence, or rather, they both sit and Emma eats, comfortably silent, but in spite of what he's let on to her, Henry remains a tangled mess of nerves. She's halfway finished when he blurts out, "You've changed," not because he thinks she has, but because he just can't take the silence anymore.

"Oh," she says. "How so?"

How so? Great, now he has to think of something. Why did he have to go and say that? Emma hasn't changed, as far as he can tell. She looks the same, walks the same, sounds the same. Hell, she even takes her coffee the same.

It hits him then, the most discomforting realization that if either of them has changed, it's him. And the thing he finds so discomforting is that he's not so sure she'll like the changes. So he skirts the topic, changes the subject. This time with something worse.

"I've missed you," he says.

"I've missed you too."

Why is she smiling? Why does she look so sad? Henry can't help but not believe her.

"You didn't have to say it, just because I said it." He smiles and waves a hand through the air, dismissively. But Emma's expression isn't so dismissive.

"Why did you say that, Henry?"

"Why did I say what?"

"That I didn't have to say it, just because you said it. Why would you think I'd do that?"

That's a hell of a good question, and it doesn't take long for the answer to come to him. "I guess I just find it hard to believe."

"Why?" Her eyes are wide, determined. There's no getting out of this one.

"You haven't always been honest with me, Emma. Not with your feelings anyway."

She leans back in the booth, considering. Henry thinks she might cry, but she doesn't. She smiles and says, "Yeah, I guess you're right." Then she says again, "Henry, I've missed you," and this time he believes it, though he knows that maybe he shouldn't.

While Henry waits for Emma to finish, to wipe the crumbs from her lips and then take a few little sips of her coffee, he thinks of the evening he actually had in mind. It hadn't looked like coffee and cupcakes at midnight, but it had certainly looked like this. Emma in front of him, smiling (sort of), a halfway delighted look on her face. When she finishes with her sad little icingless vanilla cupcake, her coffee less than halfway full, and she gives him that smile, that expectant look of hers, he starts to feel some courage swell up in him. Maybe, just maybe...

"So," he says. "I know this is sort of a backwards way of doing things, but I was thinking—"

Emma looks at him, her green eyes bright, and answers before he can ask. "Yes, Henry. I might be hungry for dinner now."

He reaches for her hand and smiles. "I thought you might be." He squeezes gently. "I'll go get the car."

"You have a car? *In the City*?"

"Crazy, huh? Parking costs almost as much as my mom's rent on the Upper West Side." He shrugs.

"Good thing you're not here that often."

"Oh, no, I don't bring it with me when I leave. I have another one on post."

Emma pauses, considering. She loosens her hand from his. "How'd you get here then?"

"Train."

She looks at him curiously, then bursts out laughing. "Henry Hayes, you are such a mystery to me."

"What can I say, Em? You're a dancer. I gotta keep you on your toes." *Lame*, he tells himself, but at least she's still smiling. He taps the table and gives her a wink. "Wait here."

It's already getting cooler outside. Nervously, Henry rattles his keys in his hands, tossing them back and forth from hand to hand. It's a ten-minute trip to his car and back, but it feels like forever.

The whole while, he can't help but wonder if, in this quick little span of time that he's gone from her, Emma sits in that bakery and thinks of him, like he thinks of her. Has she ever? Does she remember the warmth of his hand over hers, the way the corners of his eyes crinkled when he winked at her? He wonders if she's happy, for once. If she feels whole. If a smile plays across her face.

Or if maybe Henry is completely wrong about what it is that's about to happen.

CHAPTER 12

A red truck pulled up in front of the cupcake place. Two quick, polite honks. Emma made her way outside, surprised by the sight of it, though she sort of knew it had to be him. She watched in something like delighted confusion as Henry stepped down from the truck and walked toward her.

She shook her head and her lips parted, the tiniest hint of a smile. "And it's a truck," she said. "Probably the only one in all of Manhattan."

Henry took her hand in his, grinning. He walked her to the passenger's side and guided her in. "Turns out it's true, what they say. You can take the boy out of the south—"

"But he's gonna bring his pickup truck."

"Yeah," Henry said, his smile wide. "Something like that."

Traffic was a nightmare, like it always was, as they made their way across town, and the ride was especially bumpy in Henry's truck. They bounced along the avenues, down the streets, towering over the other cars. Everyone fled from their path. Every set of eyes looked at them. *What are those two country bumpkins doing in this great City?* they must have thought. Emma had never felt bigger, more awkward, so out of place. But at the same time it was all sort of perfect. It was…fun. Like, Henry fun. Like it used to be.

It was half an hour before they made it to the other side of the tunnel. Emma looked curiously at Henry. "What are we in Jersey for?"

"You said you were hungry, didn't you?"

"Yeah, but—" She looked back at the glowing lights of the City. "There's like twenty thousand restaurants in Manhattan alone."

"Really?" he said. "Last I heard it was closer to thirty."

"Henry, you know what I mean…"

He glanced her way for just a second. "What I had in mind, you can't get in the City."

"What you had in mind?"

"Right." His smile grew even more mischievous. "Don't worry, it's not much farther."

Emma nodded hesitantly. She looked out from the passenger window, rolled it down and reached out her hand.

They were up to speed now, cruising along. The air sifted through her open hand, palm-up, her fingers spread wide. She closed her eyes, felt the wind on her face, heard the music roll out from the speakers when Henry turned on the radio. When he reached his hand across the console, she allowed his fingers to slip through hers.

Then, in the comfort of this place, the wind and the music and the warmth in her hand, Emma felt a swelling within her chest and her eyes grew heavy. She allowed them to close, trying to remember the last time she'd slept. What had it been, two nights? Three? A moment later, her eyes opened. She looked at Henry.

"I didn't see where you put my bag."

He motioned behind the seat. "You should be able to reach it from there."

Emma reached for her bag and flung it across her lap, fumbling around for the notebook and the pencil inside it. Then she leaned forward and turned down the radio. "If you don't mind," she said as she opened the notebook to the next blank page.

He shook his head. "No, I don't mind."

The calm that had washed over her tonight was a familiar one, but for a very different reason.

"Wanna get high?" Henry asked.

"You're kidding, right?"

"No, not really."

"Henry, what the fuck?"

"It's no big deal," he said. "Just don't get addicted."

"Easier said than done?"

"Not for people like you, Emma. With enough self control, you'll only get addicted to the things you want to be addicted to."

"I'm not addicted to anything."

"Coffee?"

I hesitated. "Maybe."

"And dancing?"

"OK, so what? Dancing won't kill me."

"Neither will pot…in moderation. Just enjoy it. Ride out the high while it lasts. Then, when it's over, you just forget it. Don't even think of it."

"How often do you do it?"

"Not more than once a month. Sometimes twice. Sometimes just once every few months." He paused, looking at me while I listened closely. "It'll clear your head, ya know. And that might not be such a bad thing."

"Yeah, but it'll also make me forgetful."

"Pish posh. You've gotta live, Emma. Goddammit, you've gotta live a little.*"*

Part of me wanted to do it then, just so he'd stop saying that. But another part of me, a bigger part, was curious—excited, even. "We'll only do it once?"

"Just once."

"And you'll stay with me the whole time?"

"Of course."

"OK," I said. "Let's do pot."

Henry laughed. "You don't do pot, Em. You smoke it. Let's smoke pot.*"*

"I guess that's the kind of thing I would know if I'd lived a little."

Henry didn't tell me how he got it, and I didn't care to know. I knew enough already: that drugs were readily available at Academy, like alcohol and cigarettes. Pot really wasn't considered a big deal; everyone did it. Except the dancers, we didn't have that luxury. Chloe would have freaked if she knew. Apparently, Henry said, this was the "good shit" and I was in for quite a treat.

He showed me how to break apart the fluffy green herb, so innocent-looking in its natural state, then he rolled it up into a blunt. "Spit," he said.

"What?"

"To hold it together."

I grimaced. "That's disgusting."

"Just do it."

I did it. I gathered all of the spit in my mouth and shot it through my lips, onto the blunt.

"More," he said.

"More?"

"It has to close all the way. The end of it, too. So really hack it up, OK? Then you have to lick it closed."

"Why don't you do it?"

"Would you rather your spit or mine?"

"Touché." I couldn't believe I was doing this. It took so much spit to get the ends sufficiently wet, then I had to lick it to seal the ends of the cigar paper together. Not one lick across, like an envelope, but back and forth several times.

"Nice," Henry said.

"Yeah, yeah. What now?"

"I'm just saying. You're good at that."

"What do you mean?" I asked. "What am I good at?"

"Nothing," he said. "We're ready to light it. I'll go first."

Henry lit the end and took a long, deep drag, sucking it back in little bursts before inhaling and then breathing out a trail of smoke. His eyes closed for a long moment, then he opened them and smiled at me. He passed it to me and gave me a little nod.

I felt so uncoordinated, with the blunt between my fingers and the lighter in my other hand. It was hard to light with my left hand. "Maybe help me?" I asked, passing the lighter back to Henry.

"Sure." He lit the end for me while I sucked. But I couldn't feel anything. No smoke, no high. I exhaled clear air.

"It's not working."

"Suck harder."

This time I sucked as hard as I could, the smoke burning as it hit my lungs. I coughed so hard I thought it would never stop. I mean, violently coughed. I could feel every hot particle of smoke in my lungs. When it finally eased after several minutes, though not completely, a quietness settled in my chest. But little more. My mind still felt perfectly clear.

"I don't feel it."

"You will."

While I waited, Henry took another hit. I watched as his face relaxed, his bloodshot eyes nearly closed in tiny slits. He was smiling.

"*You're really high?*" I asked.

"*High as a kite.*"

"*What the fuck. Why don't I feel it?*"

"*Stop trying so hard,*" he said. "*Let it feel you.*"

"*What?*"

"*Just relax. You're not being open to it. Let it pull you in and take you under.*"

Oh my god, he is so high. *I rolled my eyes and looked away from him, and then, as I was just about to give up, I felt the wave wash over me.*

"*You feel it?*"

"*Yeah.*"

"*Good. You wanna listen to some music?*"

"*Sure.*"

"*What do you feel like listening to?*"

"*Andrea Bocelli.*"

"*Never heard of her.*"

"*Him,*" I said. "*He does an amazing rendition of* La bohème *in his latest album. It's about love and loss. You should see the opera sometime. It's the most emotionally evocative experience.*"

"*Sounds kind of boring.*"

"*It's a masterpiece.*"

"*Yeah?*" Henry turned to me and smiled. "*Let's hear it then.*"

"*Me? I'm a terrible singer.*"

"Then take me sometime."

"Okay, I will." I smiled back at Henry. He passed me the blunt and I took another hit. It went down smooth this time. I set it down and rested my head on his shoulder. I knew he would have preferred some music to accompany his experience, but I relished the quiet. After some time, I sat back up and looked over at him again. "Wanna go for a walk?"

"Sure, where to?"

"Someplace that has ice cream. I'm craving something sweet."

He looped my arm through his and hoisted me up. "I'm sure you are," he said. "I know just the place."

When we arrived, I looked at the clock. 11:45. Had it only been forty-five minutes since we started smoking? It seemed like I'd been high for hours. "Holy shit, do you see what time it is?"

"Don't holy shit me until you try this." Henry handed me a bowl of what was supposedly homemade French vanilla ice cream. I scooped a bit with a spoon and pressed it against my tongue.

"Holy mother of—"

"Amazing, right?"

"Oh my god," I said. "It's so delicious."

"Are you glad you did this with me?"

"Yes, it's been quite an experience, Henry." And it was. "I don't know how I can just forget it."

He laughed and said, "You'll be fine."

Remembering it now, I feel like that happened both yesterday, and a lifetime ago.

• • •

The road is beginning to wind. The moon is full and bright, though small and distant at this hour, and the hills start to wave on the horizon. Music pours out softly from the radio as Emma rests. She'd written furiously just minutes earlier, jotting down a flurry of thoughts, then, all of a sudden, she shut the notebook and tucked it away. Now she lies beside him, the weight of her head on his forearm, her eyes fluttering underneath their lids. The lights of the City grow dim, and the tree line thickens.

Henry drives as steadily as possible to the top of a hill he discovered just last year, when he returned from his first deployment. From the open space where the hill plateaus, he takes a deep breath. He parks the truck and turns the key, leaving the heat and the music low. He brushes a strand of hair out of Emma's face. Though she rested peacefully, she wakes up startled.

"Where are we?"

"You'll see." He walks to her side and helps her step down, then turns her around to face the bed of the truck. He asks her to close her eyes. "Wait here."

A moment later, Henry is by her side again. *Showtime.* He

places a hand over her eyes while his other hand leads her forward against the small of her back. Deep, calming breaths. "OK," he whispers. "Open."

Emma lets out her breath as she takes it all in. A table and bench; candles and hors d'oeuvres and a bottle of wine; lights wrapped around the trees and strung overhead. Music plays softly, distantly.

It's a risky move, bringing her here, doing all of this. Henry knows that. But the way he sees it, only two things can come of this. Emma will either run away, back to Manhattan (now, *fast*), or she'll step forward to the edge of the plateau and stare ahead at the lights of the City.

He knows Emma well enough by now, and he knows she couldn't care less about candles and wine and music and lights. He knows that isn't what could most impress her. It's the City that does it.

Henry doesn't realize he's holding his breath until Emma steps forward and he lets it all out. She gazes wide-eyed at the lower Manhattan skyline. Though distant, the City lights up the entire sky. It glows red, bathed in light. A wisp of a cloud blankets the moon.

"It doesn't matter how often I see it," she says. "It always amazes me."

"Yeah," Henry says, looking not at the lights of the City, not at the glowing red sky or the bright speck of a moon, but at Emma. "I know the feeling."

She stands quietly in awe for several moments until Henry breaks the silence. "I hope you're hungry," he says.

"Yes, actually." She makes her way to the table and smiles. "And everything looks perfect."

Emma sits down, her hands folded across her lap, her smile wide as she looks up at Henry, expectantly. He reaches for the bottle of wine, uncorks it, and pours her a glass. As he walks around the table to sit across from her, she places a small slice of bread and a few little squares of cheese on her plate. Her eyes remain fixed on the skyline in front of her.

Henry is proud of himself in this moment. He's gotten the girl. This most difficult girl. *Finally.* He watches as she sips the wine he poured for her, as she gazes out at the City from the top of this hill he found, as she enjoys the evening exactly the way he planned it. His heart swells. He forgets everything that isn't worth remembering right now.

"What are you thinking?"

Emma turns to face him. The wind blows through her hair, and her face is bright with the glow of lights. "I was thinking how strange it is," she says, "how I can be so hurt, so broken, by a place so beautiful."

"Oh."

She puts down her glass, her eyes set on his. "You're

wondering what happened to me," she says. She's actually smiling.

Henry shrugs, like, *Yeah, as a matter of fact, I think you have some explaining to do,* but he doesn't say anything. She could say the same about him.

"You know my father died in those towers." Her smile fades. He nods. "I just don't remember it happening. Did you know that? Did you know I'd forgotten?" He wants to say yes but she doesn't give him time to answer. Thank God, because he's just not ready to explain himself yet. How he knows that she's forgotten.

Emma goes on. "One day all was well and the towers stood tall and strong, as my father did, and the next thing I know, they are gone. And so is he."

"I'm sorry. And I'm sorry you don't remember."

She shrugs. "People say it's a blessing that I've forgotten."

"Maybe so, but I'd want to remember."

She reaches for more hors d'oeuvres and Henry wonders if he should have made something more substantial. She finishes her wine and hands him the glass. He fills it halfway.

"You must miss him terribly."

"You can't even imagine."

"Sometimes I wish I could," Henry says. "I never knew my father though. Did I ever tell you that?"

She shakes her head and leans toward him, setting down

her glass of wine. "I wondered."

"He left before I was born. He never tried to find me, not even now. Sometimes I wish I knew him, that I could have even one single happy memory with him, and that maybe I'd lost him some other way. Some tragic way, even... I know it must sound terrible," he says, "but that's how I feel. I wish I could remember him as someone who loved me."

"I guess it's better to have loved and lost then, like they say."

"Yeah. I guess you're right. I'm still so sorry."

She nods and says, "Me too," and then that hush falls over them again until Emma turns back to Henry. "Either way, it doesn't matter. What's done is done, and I practically relive it every day. Every day that I'm here, anyway. Every day that I'm in this City."

"Relive it?" he asks.

"I know it doesn't make sense. I really don't remember any of it. But then, sometimes..."

"Sometimes what?" His face warms in spite of the chill.

"Sometimes I think maybe I do remember it. I think...maybe...I was actually *there*."

Henry takes a sip of wine and swallows hard. Emma can't remember. She *can't*. Because if she remembers, if she remembers it all exactly, she will hate him. Not high school hate him, but really hate him.

So he changes the subject. "What about your mother?"

• • •

Augusta hadn't wanted to tell her, but Emma managed to tug it out of her.

Emma's mother, Frances, was eighteen when her parents divorced. It was no big deal, Augusta said. They just didn't like each other all that much, agreed they were better off as friends. It was mutual. And when Frances was all grown up, well, what was the point of them staying married? Frances hadn't seen it coming. She never saw them fight, and Emma assumed they never did. A slow and silent deterioration. Like termites.

Emma loved hearing Augusta talk about her mom. What young girl doesn't? To hear about all her mischief, the way she acted around her high school crush. Her rebellious streak. She wanted to know how she had reacted to her parents' divorce. Augusta shook her head. "I'm not entirely sure," she said. When Emma furrowed her brows, her grandmother clarified. "She never mentioned it, like it was no big deal. A non-event. I believe it was a big deal though. A very big deal. She just channeled her grief elsewhere."

"Elsewhere?" Emma asked.

"Your mother always had stars in her eyes. A week after the

official divorce, her bags were packed. She bought a one-way ticket to New York City. Blew off her scholarship to Reed College." Augusta snapped her fingers. "Just like that."

"*Reed College?*"

She nodded. "Oh, Emma, I did love your father though. They met in the City almost right away, might have even been that first week she was there, and he just swept your mom right off her feet. To be honest, I was surprised how quickly she fell in love in New York, how quickly she let herself be grounded. With that free spirit of hers."

Free spirit? That wasn't the Frances Jenkins Emma had grown up with.

It was like Augusta could read her mind. "Love can change you, Em. For better, for worse. You never can tell. You've just got to be careful, because you can't always choose who you fall in love with."

The wine was now almost completely gone. She could feel her head start to buzz. Her lips tingled a little, growing numb.

Emma told Henry what Augusta had said. It was more than a year ago, back in Tillamook. Henry looked deep in thought. "But your mother was always so—"

"Uptight?"

He smiled. "I was going for serious, but we can use your word. So what happened, exactly?"

"Well, I have a theory." Emma knocked back the last sip of her wine. This conversation would need it. "You remember my dad, right? Smart, funny, sophisticated. Old New England money."

Henry half-smiled. "Not at all intimidating."

Emma laughed. "It was a lot for my mother, this young girl from the woods of Oregon, pairing up with someone as handsome and rich as my father. She was thrust into this whole new society, you know? She had to live up. She had to fit in."

Henry nodded, considering. "Your dad was always so cool though, in spite of who he was or how much money he had. And I know I wasn't around them much, but I remember thinking how in love they seemed. Always touching."

"I don't doubt their love," Emma said. "Not one bit. And I think my father would have loved her just as much had she been true to herself. But she lost herself in him. She lost her spirit. Her *identity*."

"So when he died—"

"She was so lost, Henry. You should have seen her. Just this broken shell of a woman. She wouldn't eat. She wouldn't sleep. She hardly talked, except for these brief but instant fits of anger she had. It was months after Dad's death that my mother died too, but she was gone long before she actually passed away."

Emma could have been done with the story then, but Henry was listening intently. She knew she had to go on. Get to the end.

"I thought maybe it was depression, that thing that had crept in after my father died, swallowed up my mother and carried her through to the end of her life. She hadn't been professionally diagnosed, but what else could it have been? What else could have taken the woman she was and emptied her out, her soul filtering out of her like sand?" She paused. "I found her in her room one morning, lying in bed. Her skin wasn't pale, but gray. Her hair was spread out on the pillow beneath her head, like a yellow orb. She hadn't eaten in weeks, she was so emaciated. A tiny bird underneath the covers."

"Did she…"

Emma shook her head. "There were no signs of physical harm. We even had an autopsy performed; she hadn't ingested anything. She just sort of withered away. I thought it ironic, actually. Normally the body goes first, then the soul. But with my mom, it was all backwards."

Silence dwelt. Emma hadn't known what a heavy weight her mother's death had been until she let it out just then. Henry sat still, pondering. He turned to her and the silence lifted.

"I just can't imagine your father having that sort of effect on her. That she would lose herself in him. You really think, all that time, that she was working so hard to be someone she wasn't? Maybe that was the real her, after all. Maybe Augusta was wrong. She wasn't such a free spirit after all."

"Henry," Emma said, managing a smile, "just because you don't need to pretend around someone, doesn't mean you don't still try."

A while later, the table was emptied of food and wine. Emma felt full and buzzed. She wiped the exhaustion from her eyes.

"So what do we do now, Henry?" she said. "Now that you're all up to speed?"

He stood from the table and smiled, his hand held out toward her. "What we're best at," he said. "We dance."

She placed her hand in his, knowing it wasn't a question.

When the music slowed, so did they. Henry pulled her snug against him. "I have to say, I'm really proud of you."

Emma backed away to face him. "What do you mean?"

"After all that's happened, you don't seem bitter. Not even a little bit."

Her mouth twisted. "Bitter?"

"I don't mean to open closed wounds, Em, but it seems

like your mother could have bounced back, that she could have found a way to be whole again. After all, she might not have been a wife anymore, but she was still a mother. *Your* mother."

It wasn't the first time she'd thought of that, and Henry was right: Emma was bitter at times, but for some reason she wasn't today.

She smiled and said, "It comes in waves."

CHAPTER 13

Emma's head grows heavy on his shoulder. The music ends.

"We should head back," Henry says.

She looks up at him with tired eyes. Somehow they seem brighter. Maybe it's all the lights.

"If you'd like. But I'd rather stay. Watch the sun come up."

It's a perfect idea, but they still have hours before sunrise. "Do you want to rest a while?"

Emma nods sleepily. Henry tidies up and turns off the lights, then he takes off his jacket and lays it down. With his legs straight out in front of him, they slope downward with the hill. The trees here hang overhead like a canopy.

Emma sits on the jacket beside him with her legs tucked beneath her, her arms coiled around one of his. When she rests her head on his shoulder again, her hair drapes in front of her face, across his chest. It's soft and warm, thick copper waves kissed by the sun.

Before long, her breathing slows. She's fast asleep, but he's wide awake. Alive, *electric.* He is very aware of the blood in his veins. His heavy pulse.

How can she rest at a time like this? She must know the effect she has on him. It has to be obvious, he's never tried to hide it. The softness of her skin on his. Her lips, plump and smooth. Her wide gaze and playful smile. Tired as she might be, how can she possibly be sleeping, knowing—*knowing*—just how he feels when she's next to him?

And call him crazy, but he's starting to believe he might have a similar effect on her as well.

An hour goes by and slips into another. Emma's face was burrowed between his chin and shoulder for a while, tucked into the nape of his neck until it slid down to his chest. Now she lies with her head on his stomach, her arm slung across his waist. Henry leans back on his hands and watches her breathe. With her legs splayed out in front of her, her yellow skirt has risen a little.

He reminds himself to breathe as well.

The cloudless sky lightens faintly. The sun has taken its time this morning, but now that its rise has begun, he knows the rest will happen quickly. He runs a finger through Emma's hair, and her green eyes open.

"Mornin', sunshine," Henry says.

She scoots herself up and faces Manhattan.

"Is it?" she asks.

"Almost."

They watch in silence as the City lights flicker off one by

one, the darkness of the sky melting away as the sun burns through it. Red to orange to yellow. It becomes too bright to watch any longer.

Emma faces him with a smile. She doesn't know it, but he hasn't really planned for anything else. He tries to think of something quick, but it turns out it's a good thing he hasn't. Because Emma has made a few plans of her own.

"Let's see the statue," she says.

"The what?"

"The Statue of Liberty."

Before he knows it, she's on her feet. She reaches for his hand and pulls him up. "It's been forever since I've seen her up close."

Let me paint you a picture. It's the first time he's been on the Staten Island Ferry, and it's *cold*. Emma has his jacket, which is fine, except she doesn't seem to really need it, since it's sort of open across her chest and flapping like crazy against the wind, and the sky now looks like it's about to rain. The clouds grumble. It must have rained a little here earlier, because a few heavy drops keep spilling from the awning and onto his head, trickling down his neck. And did I mention how cold it is?

To top it all off, Henry gets motion sickness. Yeah, yeah,

some soldier he is.

The ferry begins to steadily rock. Once they're up to speed, the wind grows stronger and colder, and the frigid air doesn't help with the nausea either, as he hoped it might. Emma leans forward against the railing with her eyes closed, taking the force of the wind on her face.

"There's nothing like it," she says as she spreads out her arms. Her chin is lifted into the wind.

Right, nothing like it. This is why he didn't join the Navy.

Henry stands behind her, against the glass, hoping the awning overhead might shield him from the cold and that maybe the swaying motion of the ferry will be less intense if he backs away from the edge. It isn't, though.

"Nope," he says through gritted teeth. "Nothing like it."

Emma half turns to look at Henry. "What are you doing back there? You'll see her better from here." She reaches her hand for his.

"OK." He takes her hand and inches closer to the railing, holding his breath. Just then, this huge gust of wind whips right over them, and Emma, of all things, starts to laugh. Giddy, uncontrollable laughter. Like she's overcome with happiness.

He tries to enjoy the moment with her, but he can't. He just can't. He stands here quietly, shivering, still holding his breath, then Emma scoots closer until their shoulders touch. She looks at Henry, studying his face, and he knows exactly what she sees. That his skin has turned a waxy greenish hue and his lips are drained of color.

"You're hating this."

"No, not hating it. I just get a little seasick."

"I can see that." She slips her arms out of his jacket and hands it to him. "I'm fine without it. Really. You look like you're freezing."

Before Henry can argue, Emma presses the jacket against him, and he puts it on. He's about to zip it up when she eases herself against him, her arms wrapped around his back, nuzzling into the open flaps of the jacket. He can feel her breath, warm and steady, as her lips press against his skin.

"But now I'm just warming *you*," he says.

Emma smiles. "Yeah, well, I was a little cold too."

The air grows colder, and his nausea becomes far more intense as the ferry rocks on. But with it all comes a sort of calm, too, as Emma presses herself harder against his chest. Before long, she lifts herself off him and reaches for his hand again. She pulls him closer to the edge.

"Look, Henry! There she is!"

"Wow," he says, though he's slightly underwhelmed by the view.

"Have you ever seen her up close before?"

"Nope. Never."

"Well, what do you think?"

"She looks…smaller than I expected."

"No way," Emma says, swiping the air with her open hand. "She's *perfect*."

"And what is it you love so much about her?"

"Her strength, mostly. No matter what, she stands there, always faithful, declaring to us our freedom. She'll never turn her back on us." She takes a step forward before turning back to face him. "She'll never fail us," she says.

By now the cold and the motion are long forgotten. Henry reaches for Emma and pulls her against him again. This time, he's not so delicate.

"Neither will I, I hope you know."

"Yes, Henry. I know."

When the ferry docks at Staten Island, Henry expects Emma will want to get off and walk around a while, but she doesn't. She takes his hand and leads him up to the front of the ferry. They sit down together inside the cabin.

"You won't feel it as much from up here."

"What about you? Don't you want to see her on the way back?"

186

She shakes her head. "Just the one time. That was enough."

"You said it's been forever since you've seen her up close. When was the last time?"

"Right before my father died."

"Oh," he says. "I'm sorry."

"Don't be. It was a good memory. The four of us all came. Lois, my parents, and me. My mom went to Lois's school to pick her up, and Dad came to mine. It was a Thursday, in the middle of the day, and for no apparent reason, really. They just wanted to bring us here, to make sure we'd see her as often as we could."

"That's as good a reason as any to skip school," Henry tells her. "It seemed like you guys did that a lot."

Emma laughs. "They were always doing stuff like that. Finding excuses to get us out of school. I know they came off as serious and uptight, and they sort of were about a lot of things. In a way, this was just another one of those things they were so strict about. We had to go out and make memories together. We *had* to."

Henry smiles. "You were quite a family, Emma."

"Yeah, we were. We really were." She looks out toward Manhattan and smiles before turning back to face him. "And what about you, Henry? You lived in the City for a while, and apparently you still come back all the time. Did you ever come here with your family?"

"I thought about it. I know my sister would have loved it. Remember Laura?" Emma nods. "She never got to come here. I wish I would've brought her here, but I never did. I guess time just sort of...slips ahead of you."

"What do you mean? Why can't you bring her now?"

"Right, I guess I never told you." He breathes deeply, but it's not as hard to say as he thought it would be. "Laura died a year ago. She and her husband. They were in a car accident."

"Oh, Henry. I'm so sorry."

"It's OK," he tells her. "I have so many good memories. And Tabby...I just thank God she wasn't with them." He pauses before saying, "It's OK," again, and he almost wonders if it really is.

"You should bring her here," Emma says. "You should bring Tabby here. Unless, of course, you don't think you can stomach it." She manages a teasing smile.

"That's an idea, but I think maybe you're right...about the stomach thing. If it's OK with you then, you might have to bring her for me. If it's OK with you," he says again.

"Yeah," she says. "That might be OK."

Henry's chest expands when the ferry finally docks in Manhattan. Immediately upon their return, Emma takes his hand and tugs him forward.

"There's another thing I want to show you," she says. "But first, we need to find us a little something warmer." She's still in her yellow skirt and thin green sweater, but Henry knows she's perfectly comfortable—that *us* really just means *you*. Man, does he feel like a baby.

It's not so bad though.

Downtown, Emma leads him into a small shabby-looking clothing store. "I know it doesn't look like much, but I've been coming here for years. Before…well, you know." She skirts past it. "It's the best quality and service in Manhattan. I swear by it."

"I trust you." Henry watches as Emma flutters away from him and walks around the store. He doesn't follow, since he's completely out of his element, and he knows she isn't about to carry him along. So he just hangs back, loitering around near the front entrance, taking in the musty smell of leather and the bustle of people that stride in and out of the store. He waits patiently, though he's a little worried about what Emma will return with.

After several minutes, she reappears from the racks holding a coat in each of her hands.

"Wool or fleece?"

He looks them over. Neither is half bad, actually, but he'll be out of here long before he'll need something as heavy as wool. He points to the fleece one.

Emma tosses the wool coat to the side and steps behind him with the other.

"Let's see," she says, guiding his arms into the coat.

It drops to his shoulders like a dream. Perfect fit. He smiles at Emma in approval, and she smiles back.

Good. Done. Now we can go.

Or so he thinks, but Emma is still looking him over, studying every angle of the coat. She walks up to him, and he could swear she has that look in her eyes like she might be coming in to wrap her arms around him again, maybe even go for a kiss. But he can't imagine that happening now, in a place like this, surrounded by people and coats, with the heavy glare of the salesman from across the store.

As Emma steps closer, her arms remain crossed over her chest, her expression serious. She walks around him, smoothing out the lines on his shoulders, running her hands down his arms and back. She turns him around to face her, then reaches her hands to his neck. He can feel the tingle of her fingertips on his skin as she folds the collar down, then she buttons him up and places her hands on his chest, ensuring the fit.

"Perfect," she says, patting down the fabric. Her smile is luminous.

When Emma steps back, she takes his hand in hers, entangling their fingers as they walk toward the register.

"Now you're ready for the bridge," she says.

Henry looks at her curiously, then he glances outside. Has she seen what's happening with the weather?

She smiles coyly. "If you thought it was cold on the ferry, just you wait."

• • •

As they made their way to the Brooklyn Bridge, the wind picked up and the air grew colder. Though it was nearing October, already it seemed like winter was rolling in, clutching the City with its icy hand. Emma wasn't fazed. She turned to Henry.

"I have to show it to you."

At the base of the bridge, her heavy stride came to a halt. She looked up and inhaled deeply, her entire being in a state of pause. It hit her, sharp and quick, that heavy sadness again, and for a moment she didn't think she could do it. She wished she could fold herself inward again—just be in herself, wholly, entirely, impenetrable. But it wasn't possible now. Why had she brought him here? What was she thinking?

Now there was no going back.

Henry didn't say a word. He stood close, allowing her arm

to snake through his. It took several moments before Emma was ready to speak again, but the moment did finally come. An equal and opposite force from the sadness.

"Something happened here, Henry. Something you should know."

"OK." He nodded. "I knew you had something to tell me, Em. There's no need for secrets. Not for us. Tell me what happened."

Emma looked back as if someone were watching. A ghost. As the wind came she moved a ringlet of her hair behind her ear. There were his hands. She placed hers in one of his.

"Come. I'll show you."

It was a long walk up, steeper than she remembered, and the weather continued to deteriorate. The clouds were rolling quickly now. The rain moved over them like an angered wisp. They felt unsteady, with the wind whipping relentlessly against their faces and the ground slippery beneath their feet. Heavy traffic thundered past them. They were alone.

Henry was shouting to Emma even though he stood right next to her. "Are you sure it's safe?"

"Yes, I'm sure!"

When they made it halfway over, Emma stopped abruptly. "Here," she said. She stood against the edge, facing out toward the river. She knew her face had grown pale, and she began to

192

shiver. The rain was drenching now, but she didn't care. Emma stood soaking wet, her hair in disarray, makeup running down her face.

"What is it?" he urged.

She faced away from him as she spoke. "Not long after my father died, sometime before I left for Oregon, I came here. I stood right here, in this very spot. And for one reason only. There's only one reason why I came here that night."

"Go on," Henry said.

Emma's voice grew louder. "I came here to end it, Henry! It was late at night and no one was around, just like now. And it was raining too. It was wet and blustery, like today, and it would have been so easy! I wouldn't have even been seen." Her eyes filled with tears and her voice became strained, her words choked. "I wouldn't have been looked for, either. No one would've come searching for me. Not for a long while. It would have been like I'd just vanished."

Henry didn't speak. He just placed his arms around her and pulled her close.

She went on, her tears pooling on the fabric of his coat. "It's awful, I know. But I missed him so much. I couldn't live without him, and for so long I hated myself that I couldn't do it. I hated that I wasn't brave enough to go to him."

As she poured out her confession, Henry remained calm and quiet. Patient. "What stopped you?" he said.

"I was too afraid to jump. I came all the way here and I climbed up over the railing, onto one of those beams that stretches high above the traffic. I leaned forward and braced myself, felt the roar of the cars beneath me. But in that moment I just couldn't do it. It was fear that stopped me, nothing else. I wasn't thinking of anyone but me. Not Mom, not Lois. I know you must think I'm so awful—"

"I don't," he said as he tugged her closer. "I think you're incredible, actually. I think you have a great deal to live for. You know that now, don't you?"

Emma didn't answer. She let the weight of her body grow heavy against his as they stood together. The seconds passed slowly.

It was Henry who broke the silence.

"Emma?" he said.

"Yeah, Henry?"

"What made you decide to tell me this?"

She gazed up at him with wide eyes. "Because, I…"

He held her face in his hands. "Tell me, Emma. Just say it."

"Because I love you, Henry. I'm in love with you." The words silenced them both, and her body felt frozen. Numb. What had she done? Had she so easily forgotten what had happened the last time?

But now Emma was sure he loved her too. Even more so,

if it were possible, than she was before. The time he hadn't said it back. An anxious swelling burned within her as she waited. It shattered the numbness, the cold. She could feel the hammering of her heart in her chest, and nothing else.

Only after several breaths did Henry move, and when he did, he brushed the clumps of soaking, matted hair away from her face and wiped the mascara from her tear-stained cheeks. His hands lingered. He lifted her chin toward him.

"Say it again," he said.

"I love you."

He leaned in closer, his hands cradled around her neck. "Say it again." His voice was soft. His pulse quickened against her skin. "Say it again."

"I love you, Henry."

Finally, he smiled. "You know I love you too."

"Yes," Emma said, letting out a heavy breath. "Now I do."

The wind howled, and the rain was showering down on them now. Ripples coursed through the river, ebbing wildly below them, and the bridge subtly rocked beneath their feet. But everything was still, too. The world was quiet. There was just Henry, this man who loved her, who allowed his gaze to fall on hers as she leaned into him, tangled up in his embrace.

Then, in the quickest instant, the burning, anxious swelling began to spread. Desire. *Urgency.* She could feel his eyes on every part of her. Cheeks, eyes, lips. His stare traced the soft lines of her neck, her shoulders, and her chest. His hands softened against her face before drifting slowly down her arms, settling into the slender curve of her waist. Their gaze was heavy as they stood, silently and still.

The seconds, they lasted for hours.

And then they slammed together. Henry lifted her up to his waist, her arms and legs flinging around him, quickly, firmly. He pressed his lips to hers, salty and slick from the rain, releasing the passion that had been surging inside of him too. They sunk into each other. His hands reached for her hair and gripped, and her long legs dropped to their sides. A trail of kisses down her neck later, and Henry's face was gone from her view. He'd released the fistfuls of her hair from his hands and spun her around by the waist.

"No, Henry."

It was like he'd gone deaf. Here she was again, precariously facing toward the river, wind and rain pelting her skin. This time she felt the hardness of Henry behind her. He lifted the hem of her skirt.

"Henry! No!"

He took her forcefully. Not just her lips this time, but the whole of her. Emma screamed when he entered, but she did not cry. The pain was both excruciating and redeeming. She stopped resisting and let him have her.

When it was over, Emma turned. She smoothed her skirt and let the weight of Henry fall against her as he breathed heavily. He lifted his head and kissed her for a long moment, and the tension in their bodies faded. After, they walked in deafening silence, their fingers entwined, the rest of the way across the Brooklyn Bridge.

The next time, it would happen more gently.

• • •

By the time they reach Brooklyn, the rain has already slowed. It's almost noon and the sun is just beginning to peek out through still ominous clouds in the center of the sky. The warmth is subtle, but enough for them to shed their outer layers.

Hungry, they stop by Grimaldi's on Front Street and order a pizza to go. Two cokes. They make their way to the promenade and lay down their jackets on a damp bench, then they sit and eat in the comfortable silence facing out toward downtown Manhattan. The breeze is steady. Sunlight glistens off the buildings and the river. The promenade is quiet, but the people will start to gather here soon as the day continues to unfold and the benches dry, the warmth of the sun swelling.

They say nothing about the bridge.

After some time, when Emma is finished eating and she's

brushed the crumbs from her hands and set down her plate, her stare becomes fixed once again on the gaping hole in the City's skyline, below which Henry knows they've just broken ground on what will someday be called the Freedom Tower.

He's not here with her though, in this moment. He feels so distant, he might as well be a hundred miles away. Because things aren't as they seem. He's lying by omission here. Why hasn't he told her yet? What's the worst that could happen? He could lose her. She could hate him. And would that be worse than this heavy burden of guilt he's been carrying? This guilt—of what he knows, of what he's done, of all this time he's held the truth from Emma—is suffocating. But she looks happy now. Truly content. Even in this state of hers. Quiet, withdrawn, even a little bit sad. It's a natural state for Emma. She is wholly herself, right now, in this moment, but it's all so fragile too. Emma. The moment. As if in any instant, with just the slightest movement in the wrong direction, the wrong word said the wrong way in the wrong second, this thing they have going now, *this moment*, will all begin to crumble. No, to shatter. Like falling glass. It's inevitable. And the worst of it is he could have avoided it. He could have dropped the glass three years ago when it had been mere inches above the ground, and they would have been fine. They could have bounced back. Right?

Now, it's like he's standing at the top of the Empire State Building, cradling the glass in his open hands, his palms slippery, and he knows he has to drop it, and that it will shatter, become something unrecognizable, irreparable, the pieces strewn across the streets of the City.

Too willingly, Henry passes it off to Emma. "Penny for your thoughts."

Her answer rushes out of her and for just a little while, Henry's relieved. Emma's voice is steady, even and soft, almost sweet-sounding. The words cut through him like knives.

"It wasn't just my dad who died in those towers," she says. "It was the entire nation, in a way. It was everything we stood for, freedom and power and strength. It was all that defined us, built up tall and gleaming, piercing through to the heavens. How had we allowed this to happen? How had we not seen it coming?"

She pauses, turning to face Henry. When he nods, though hesitantly, she continues.

"And so, as the towers came crumbling down, there my whole world went right down with them. Dancing, Juilliard. It was all reduced. Nothing remained. Nothing but a thick, heavy cloud of smoke and ashes and dust."

He should tell her how sorry he feels for her now, how he wishes it had never happened, and especially not to *her*, but he knows she would hate that. He should reach for her hand and grip it in his, but he knows *he* would hate that. Because who is he to be the one who comforts her now, when it's sort of his fault she can't remember?

He almost wishes she would just stop. He almost wishes she had moved past it already, or that it had never happened, that things could somehow be normal between them.

He realizes quickly that he's actually getting angry with her. It's hurting him—seeing her this way, hearing her go on and on. Realizing, heavily, just how hard it's been for her. And thinking, maybe, that he could have stopped it from getting so bad. She isn't finished.

"I'm not usually this melodramatic, but don't you see? This was the worst thing I'd seen in my lifetime, the first big event to make this sort of history. Every tragic moment before it was practically fiction, a product of movies and books. Not real people. Not real families with fathers, mothers, and children. Not real love and loss and *pain*.

"But there I was, really real, and right there in the middle of it all. It was like the entire earth had shifted, yet there I remained, right there in the same place I had always been. And I remember thinking I was the only one in the world who would ever really know me. And that I could never, ever say it out loud. Because I knew how people would respond: *You're still just a kid.*"

She pauses briefly, squinting up at the sun, then staring unseeing at the river in front of them. Henry doesn't say anything, because what could he say to her now? She's hardly making sense anymore. Her thoughts seem so disconnected.

"Well, I'm not just a kid anymore. I can see how some people might think so, especially in Tillamook. I wanted to start over in Oregon. I wanted to know absolutely *no one*. And I don't, really. No one but Augusta and Charles and Lois. Everyone else? They don't know me. Not the *real* me. They don't know the girl who just can't seem to find her place, the girl who'd rather cry herself to sleep and dream the world away than be awake and aware and so fully—" She stops, searching, and then: "*Alive.*"

When she glances back at him, Henry still has his eyes toward her, still sits listening intently despite her rambling.

"They don't really know me, Henry," Emma says again. She shifts herself away from him and points out across the river. "They don't know the girl whose father is still buried beneath the rubble of that second tower."

Her final words hit him with a silent *whoosh* and he can feel something ignite within him. What is it that's burning so violently? Anger? Fear? An explosion of guilt?

His hands open. The glass slips.

PART THREE

CHAPTER 14

Henry's confession whirls around in the pit of his stomach before bubbling up and boiling over.

"What's the matter, Henry?"

He turns to face her and says, "It's my fault you can't remember. Your last memories of him died along with his body. Because of me."

Her face twists. "He died because of *them.*"

"So you remember?"

"Remember what?"

"Being there."

"Being…" The word lingers. Emma stands up and hovers over him. Her creamy complexion is suddenly the color of uncooked bacon; Henry can almost hear the heat of her anger sizzling beneath her skin. He backs away instinctively as if something's about to pop up and burn him.

"Henry, what are you saying?"

"That you were there!" Henry jumps to his feet so he and Emma are face to face, and nearly nose to nose as well. He examines their stance; she's taller than he remembers… He brushes the thought away. Then, furiously, he lets more words tumble out.

"You came to me after. You were a wreck, so filthy. I knew it was bad, but I didn't know... Goddammit. I didn't know how bad it was. I hardly recognized you, but you recognized me, I think. We talked for a bit, frantically, your words were so rushed. Later, you fainted. The doctors said something about shock."

They hold their ground. Emma's face drains of color, taking on a paleish, blueish hue. He imagines this is what she'll look like when she's dead too. Is she about to pass out, he wonders? But she stands steady as mortar. Henry's feet are shoulder-width apart, arms by his sides, defensively. For a moment he considers reaching out to touch her, but he can feel his fingers shaking a little. He fists his unsteady hands and holds his mouth together tightly.

They are frozen, eyes locked. She said she's forgotten, but Henry can practically see the images flash through her mind. Was that all it took to make her remember? Her eyes flitter away from his, just for a moment, then return with a confused expression. What is she thinking? What does she know?

"Do you remember now?"

Emma's face changes quickly again. That anger. *Cooked* bacon. Her clenched hand lands solid on his cheekbone, stunning them both.

"*Fuck you, Henry.*"

• • •

Alone and fuming, Emma found her way back to Manhattan and wandered around for a while before making her way into Chloe's studio. The mere thirty-foot square space with ten-foot ceilings, stark white walls and parquet floors with rich mahogany inlays was exactly as she'd left it, with one big difference: now it was full of young, slender, bright-eyed girls. Students.

Chloe acknowledged her with a slight nod and a quick, busy smile as Emma rushed across the front of the room to the little office in the far corner. There, she was greeted by a small, smartly dressed grey-haired woman with ocean-deep blue eyes and a smile that lit up the whole room—though it was hardly bigger than a closet. Emma's heart sank. The woman who looked up brightly at Emma was Henry's mom.

As if jolted by the unspoken kindness that emanated from the woman's smile, Emma's anger melted away. She stood up tall, but her shoulders hunched slightly in defeat.

"Emma…" The woman's voice trailed off.

"Ms. Hayes."

Henry's mom was sitting in a black swivel chair in front of a makeshift desk while Emma stood just a few feet away from her, under a door frame which lacked a door. While she stood, Emma caught sight of the enormous black and white photographs of couples, young and old, as they danced. There were nearly a dozen of them, all framed and arranged neatly on the walls of the tiny room-closet.

They were lovely, Emma thought.

The two women would have said more in that moment, perhaps, were it not for the commotion that was unfolding in the background. Emma's attention turned to the class that was in session, but her gaze returned to Ms. Hayes's and held onto it while she listened.

"I can't do it!" shouted the voice of a young pouty-lipped girl.

"Yes you can," came Chloe's voice.

"I look stupid."

"No you don't."

"Dancers are supposed to be pretty! I'm too sloppy. I look ugly when I dance."

"Amy, you are beautiful—"

But the girl, inconsolable, was already on the verge of tears. "I'll never be able to do it right!"

Henry's mom stood up and walked closer to Emma. She held out her arms in an embrace which Emma relented into. Then the woman stepped back a little and placed her hands on Emma's face, a gesture Emma had seen her do to Henry numerous times before. She was smiling radiantly.

"Henry was hoping to see you before he left," she said.

"Left? He's leaving?"

"Yes…for his next deployment. Surely he told you…"

Emma stepped back. "No! Nothing—"

The room went dark. Emma jumped, startled, but turned around when she heard Chloe speak in a sing-song kind of whisper that soothed. "Amy, you can do it."

"But it's dark," the little girl said. "Why did you turn off all the lights? Now I can't see you."

"So *we* can't see *you*. You can dance from within. No one is watching, so it's not a performance. It's an emotion now, Amy. You just have to feel it."

The darkness was thick and the room was silent except for the deep inhalations and the slightest pitter-patter of the little girl's feet while she danced. Though it was dark, Emma could tell no one had moved, not even slightly.

After several minutes, the lights came back on. Amy stood in the middle of the dance floor looking sad. She lifted her eyes up slowly to her instructor.

"Class dismissed," Chloe said smiling, her arms crossed over her chest.

The students remained still for another long moment, then they gathered their things and left the studio in a flood of tutus. While Chloe was prolifically tidying up, Emma caught her arm and turned her so they were face to face.

"Did Henry tell you he was deploying?"

"Wait just a minute," Chloe said. "You have to see this." She slipped her arm from Emma's encircled fingers and clutched her hand, leading her back into the office. There, Ms. Hayes stepped aside and stood in the corner, smiling knowingly.

"What is it?" Emma asked.

Chloe sat down and faced the computer. "We had security cameras installed a few weeks back."

"And...?"

"Nighttime mode," said Ms. Hayes.

Emma looked back at Henry's mom, then turned to Chloe again. "You lied to her?"

"I had to," Chloe said, clicking away on the mouse. She pulled up the recent video footage from the security camera which, Emma could see now, hung unobtrusively in the far corner of the main room behind her. "Look."

It was brilliant. The quality of the security camera's nighttime mode was only so-so, but you could tell Amy was stunning. She performed her routine without error, perfect and beautiful. Emma wondered when Chloe might show her the video. *If* she would. She imagined the little girl's face when she saw it, a mixture of excitement and disbelief. Emma hardly believed it herself. How could Amy have so much doubt? If only she could see this.

When it was over, Chloe turned to Emma. She looked proud of what she'd just watched, but she was hardly shocked. She had done this before.

"What did you say happened with Henry?" Chloe asked. "Something you wanted to talk about?"

Emma shook her head. "No, it was nothing."

She turned to leave, acknowledging Ms. Hayes with another little smile before she walked away. Henry's mom smiled back.

"Your lips," she said as Emma passed by her. "I remember you used to fold them like that."

Emma let go with a nod and turned. "I know, it's a terrible habit." She turned and left.

Emma's mind raced, but she felt settled somehow. Calm. Relishing the way the cool air mixed with the warmth of the sun that stubbornly made its way down into the City, Emma walked back to Chloe's apartment. There, a thought struck her: it was her home now.

She walked up the steps. Something was there, sitting impossibly on the stoop. It was wrapped nearly the same way her grandmother had wrapped it before Emma left for New York: the video camera. But how? Henry?

He must have—

It didn't matter. Emma scooped up the package and tore it open once again. A letter was attached. She ran her fingers along the crease, then opened it furiously. It read:

Emma,

It's hard to know how much you remember or which of your memories are gone forever. I hope you'll forgive me for breaking in to your old apartment. I'm not sure what compelled me to do it, but I'm glad I did. Even if you get pissed at me for it. Most of your stuff was burnt to a crisp. This camera wasn't. It must be important, and so is the truth. So here goes.

You weren't in school that morning and I knew why, though I didn't think of it until they got us all to be quiet and turned on the TV. One of the towers had been hit, I forget which one. I had also forgotten which one your dad worked in. I figured he'd be safe though, until we all watched the second plane fly in. It was the most horrific thing. Everyone started talking about terror. About hate. I thought of you.

You told me that morning that you'd be going to see your dad and you'd be late. Something about a big fight. I had to leave. I had to get out of that fucking school so I could find you.

They tried to stop me but I was ruthless. I made it in time. Everything was mayhem. So many people. You looked at me and said, "Henry?" like you didn't recognize me. I said yeah and you said, are you rescuing me? I nodded at you, expecting a smile. Ridiculous, I know. You looked like a zombie, so dazed, walking slow. I tugged you forward and we ran.

Suddenly your face looked even more stricken. You said, "My dad! We have to go back for him." Emma, I'm sorry, there's no going back. That's what I said. I hoisted you up on my back and ran like hell with everyone else.

We made it about a half a mile before the South Tower collapsed. Second to get hit, first to fall. That was the one, you said. That's where your dad worked. For a second I couldn't stop staring. In a way it was the most beautiful sight. The rawness of it. Human destruction. The realization that anything could crumble.

212

The hospital in Brooklyn was total chaos. By the time we made it you were exhausted. We were both covered in soot, and we stunk like hell. The nurses told me you were dehydrated. When they laid you down your heart started to slow, like now it could. You were in shock, they said. Then you slipped into a coma. You had been slipping the whole way there, it seemed. And then it happened all at once.

You woke up later, very briefly. I'd had enough time to know what I had to do. I had to leave you. There was talk of war almost immediately, and I thought you'd be better off without me anyway. I knew you wouldn't approve of me joining the army, so I made up a story to tell you instead. One where I don't leave to fight, where I don't leave you when you might possibly need me the most. I told you I went back to Albuquerque. Nice, peaceful Albuquerque. My kind of town, right? I told you to forget me, to follow your dreams. I told you I didn't love you.

What do they say? The road to hell is paved with good intentions? I guess we'll call it that. Good intentions. I don't know, those intentions sound pretty shitty to me right now. I don't need you to forgive me though. I just need you to remember everything, and I need you to know that I love you.

I love you, Emma. I love you, I love you. I always will.

Yours,

Henry

She didn't think twice. Inside the apartment, Emma cleared a space on the TV stand in the living room and set down the camera, facing the couch. She pulled back her tempestuous hair—frizzy and wild by this point—in a tight ponytail, then she slipped off her little green sweater and smoothed down the front of her skirt. Her memories had begun to unfold behind her eyes, and she kept pushing them away. Not anymore.

For the last time, Emma approached the camera. Turning it on as she cleared her throat, she pressed record.

CHAPTER 15

Monday, September 10th
6:45 pm

He wasn't old, but that wasn't reason enough for me not to call him an old man.

It was warm and breezy, exactly as it should have been this time of year in New York City. The four of us sat on the terrace outside. My mom poured two glasses of wine and set them on the table. She scooped ice cream into two bowls: one for me, and one for Lois. We made little conversation as we looked out at the City around us. The sky above was blue and clear as the sun began to set, its final beams of light shining back at us from the buildings downtown. Mom and Dad kissed their glasses together and smiled. Lois and I dug into our ice creams, hurrying to finish before they melted.

Lois wasn't so tiny anymore. She was already seven—*seven!*—and she'd just started the second grade. I was a senior at Academy, practically a grownup, and I couldn't have been more nervous about my final year.

Or perhaps I could have been; my dad surely was. While Mom was excited for me—always wanting to hear how my Juilliard auditions were coming along, and what were my friends planning to do after high school?—Dad was beside himself with worry, fear, anxiety…all those things a parent experiences as they watch their children grow. I knew he loved me, and I knew how proud he was of the woman I was becoming. But a part of him (a *big* part of him) wanted to keep me sheltered, keep me all to himself, forever his little girl.

Old habits die hard, as they say, and though I had already changed in so many ways—from my almost-curvy waist to my painted red lips—some things hadn't changed yet. And in my mind, it was time they did.

Two empty bowls of ice cream sat on the table, and the sky turned an inky blue. Mom and Dad grew lost in conversation, laughing and smiling, as she poured him another glass of wine. Lois pulled her knees to her chin and sighed from both boredom and a full belly. As if on cue, our parents shared a knowing glance and nodded.

"What'll it be tonight?" Dad asked. "Cards or checkers?"

A groan escaped from the back of my throat. "I think I'll just go up to my room," I said. I had just turned seventeen—way too old for family Game Night.

Three sets of eyes glared at me with disapproval.

"But, honey," my mother said, masking her anger with sadness in her soft, sweet voice, "you love Game Night. And besides, this is a family activity, and you're part of the family." She gave me a nod and a smile, what would have been a motherly, condescending pat on the knee had she not been sitting on the other side of the table.

Another groan. "But Mom, I—"

"Sweetheart," Dad said, "your mother's right." Oh, why did he have to say *that*? It was so much harder to argue when they teamed up together. "But if you'd like, I'll let you choose the game for us this time."

Lois's mouth fell open. "Hey, that's not fair!" She crossed her arms tight and pouted her lips.

"You can choose next week," Mom said. "How's that sound?"

Lois relented with a shrug of her shoulders. "OK, I guess."

I slid my chair away from the table and schlepped huffily into the house. It wasn't so much that I didn't like Game Night anymore, and I did enjoy spending time with my family, but I felt like I'd been put in my place. I felt...*forced*. I felt overwhelmingly like a grownup already, and yet, somehow, at the same time, I still felt like a child too.

I was leaning inside the closet upstairs where we kept the games when I heard heavy footsteps approach me from behind. I didn't have to turn to know it was Dad. "What now?" I asked. Demanded, really. When did I become such a bitch?

He should have yelled at me then. He should have grabbed me by my arms and turned me around, forced me to look him in the eyes while he reminded me that I was still his daughter, that he was my father and he deserved my respect. That he would not stand to be treated this way. But he didn't. Instead he gave me a gentle tap on the shoulder and motioned me into my room. I followed him in and sat down on the foot of the bed, fully expecting him to stand over me with a long, tedious lecture. But again, he didn't.

Dad pulled a chair out from under the desk and slid it close to me, then he sat down with his shoulders hunched, his arms relaxed across his lap. His blue eyes looked gray and sad. Calmly, he said, "Talk to me, Emma. What's going on?"

"Nothing," I spat.

"Emma…"

Immediately, I burst into tears. I'm embarrassed to say that all it ever took to make me cry was a disappointed look from my father. Just one look.

He got up from the chair and sat next to me, placing an arm around me, and I melted into him, choking on my sobs like a little girl. Only after several minutes did the crying finally stop. I breathed deep and wiped the tears from my face. Dad unwrapped me from his embrace and inched back over to the chair in front of me. He didn't have to ask the question again; I knew he was still waiting for my answer.

"I'm seventeen," I said. "I don't want to be treated like a kid anymore."

A slight nod, but no words. No further questions. He wasn't ready for me to finish yet.

"I'm too old for Game Night."

He nodded again, this time with a curious look on his face. "You really think so?"

"Yeah."

"Am *I* too old for Game Night?"

"No, but—"

"Don't you like spending time with us?" Oh, *great*, slap on the guilt.

"Yes, but—"

"Then what is it, Em?"

"I don't want to feel like I have to. I want to choose for myself whether I play or not."

He didn't nod this time. Instead, Dad leaned in closer to me and looked me straight in the eyes. He placed his hand over mine and said, "Fair enough. You choose." He gave me a moment to process and then he asked, "Would you like to participate in Game Night tonight, young Emma?"

Young Emma. It was a nickname he'd used ever since I could remember, one that never bothered me until this very moment. In spite of the fact I sort of did want to play, I shook my head. "Not tonight, old man." Of course, it was the first time I'd ever used that particular nickname for *him*.

Dad patted me on the shoulder, stood up from the chair and nodded again. "OK," he said. "I understand." Then he turned around and left.

Tuesday, September 11ᵗʰ
7:15 am

The sun was already shining through my bedroom window by the time I woke up. I was late for school, with a throbbing headache and a sickness in my stomach. I felt terrible for the way I left things with my dad, for not sucking it up and spending time with my family.

I'd heard them laughing as they played through the night, way past Lois's bedtime, and I'd never felt lonelier as I lied awake in my bed, wishing I hadn't caused such a senseless rift between them and me. Wishing I could swallow my pride for once.

I slammed my hand down on the snooze button for the hundredth time that morning, just as my bedroom door flew open. I knew it would be Mom, that she'd enter my room in a flurry of spirits, unplug the alarm and then strip the sheets off of me.

"I know, I know," I grumbled, the alarm clock rattling as she pulled the plug from the wall, white sheets billowing above my face. "I'm getting up."

"You're late *again*, Emma. You just missed the bus, and I'm not taking you this time."

I sat up and let my legs fall over the side of the bed. My feet were cold as they touched the floor.

"I'll just take the subway then," I said as I scooted past her, scurrying across the hall to the bathroom.

When I returned, she was sitting at the foot of the bed, organizing the papers and books in my backpack. I let out an irritated sigh at the sight of an orange cotton dress that lay next to her, along with a matching cardigan, a belt, and brown shoes on the floor beneath the ensemble.

She glowered at me disapprovingly. "You know how I feel about you taking the subway. You're not old enough yet—"

"I *am* old enough, Mother!"

I pulled the dress over my head and slipped my feet into the shoes. "I'm in high school, remember? I'm a *senior*. Everyone my age takes the subway."

With a huff, she handed me the backpack. "We'll discuss this later. Breakfast is on the table."

7:45 am

Going to school would have been futile.

For one, I was already fifteen minutes late. That was enough time for Professor Linden, my first period theater instructor, to mark me absent. And there was no way she was going to change that mark after fifteen minutes of unexcused lateness. She was nearly seventy and had never been married, and you can only imagine the rumors of *why* that swirled around campus. Let's just say, Professor Linden was not the most pleasant old lady any of us had ever known.

Today would also be the day that the senior class would gather in the gymnasium to discuss plans for the homecoming parade. The meeting was scheduled to kick off sometime in the middle of second period, and would probably last until around lunchtime. What would be the theme? How many volunteers would we need? When and where and how often would we have to meet? It was a meeting for an event I had absolutely zero interest in.

Perhaps the most convincing reason for me to skip school that day was the uneasiness that continued to ebb and flow inside my stomach. I was still pining over the events from the previous evening, still queasy with regret. I wouldn't be able to concentrate in any of my classes. Not until I'd made things right with my father first. It was, quite possibly, the most intelligent decision I'd ever made.

I made it to the South Tower of the World Trade Center by 8:30 that morning where Dad was up in a conference room in the hundred-and-something floor. I tried not to make a habit of visiting him at work, but this was important and he would understand. And he did. He greeted me with a hug and a smile.

"You're looking chipper this morning, kiddo. Do something different with your hair?"

"I suppose I am," I said. "And no, this is how it always looks."

He took me to his office, where his assistant poured me a cup of coffee. He had until 9:00 to visit with me, just twenty minutes or so, then I'd have to go to school. Okay, I said.

Dad's office was filled with pictures—mostly ones of me and Lois. "Is that from our trip to Vail?" I asked, spotting a frame on the windowsill behind him.

"You said that was the most fun you'd ever had." Dad grinned. "Probably because I fell on my butt every time we did the blue slope." We laughed together.

There was a loud *bang* and the lights in his office started to flicker. Not so much that it scared us though. You always hear crazy noises in New York. It startled me just enough to jump up out of my seat before the noise quieted and the lights were steadily on again, and that just made us laugh harder.

Then Dad's office door flew open and his assistant walked in again, her face stricken. She said there was an explosion in the North Tower, barely more than a hundred feet away from us. "We have to leave now." There was a seriousness in her voice, but she was calm. Everyone was.

Dad stood up and took my hand, leading us to the stairwell. Everyone was so cordial as we made our descent, just talking small-talk, checking their phones for service. Sending texts. It was like a fire drill at school. So mundane.

"I remember the bombing in '93," my dad said. "This is nothing."

At the 90th floor, the stairwell door was propped open. There was a window facing the North Tower, and all you could see was this massive hole. Just blackness. Dad's grip on my hand tightened. The building was eviscerated.

"I want to go home," I said. All of a sudden I was so afraid. I wanted Dad to take me home where we'd be safe and he could hold me. I could be his little girl. To hell with last night. I wasn't ready to be a grownup yet.

Others froze, but we left quickly. We got to about the 80th floor when we saw Dad's assistant sitting in the corner between two flights of stairs. She was holding her ankle, writhing in pain.

Without speaking, Dad scooped her up and flung her onto his back. He piggybacked her until we reached the 78th floor, where it looked like a hundred people were waiting for the express elevator down to the lobby.

Dad's assistant was fit and pretty but still must have weighed a hundred and thirty pounds at least, and Dad was no gym rat. He was perspiring and breathing heavy, so he stopped. "It'll be fine," he told me. "We'll wait."

"I want to stay with you," I said, not because I was tired like he was. Those twenty-something flights felt like nothing so far.

"I know, but it's better that you just keep going. Trust me." And I did. I trusted him to make sure nothing bad would ever happen to me. I trusted him to save the woman. I trusted him to fucking stay alive.

"I'll meet you in the lobby," I said.

We hugged and kissed and said I love you. Then I walked back.

I was on the 74th floor when an earthquake struck. At least that's what it felt like. The steps undulated like ocean waves and the handrails blasted from the walls. A burst of heat swelled over us and the building started to sway, back and forth, so much that I nearly felt seasick. There was the pungent smell of jet fuel.

No one screamed. No one said anything. Just silence.

All of the people picked up their pace, even though everyone was so tired. They started coaching each other, the young ones helping the elderly. There was even some laughter over our precarious situation. Had we ever seen so many pairs of women's shoes in one place? Men's briefcases? Abandoned electronics?

We saw the firefighters about one third of the way down. They passed us on their way up. You could see on their faces that they knew: they were going up to fight a fire they could not stop, try to save people they could not save. They were running to their deaths.

Later, a security guard was singing "God Bless America" and I thought, am I on the Titanic or something? Is the ship going to sink?

We couldn't exit through the lobby; we had to go through the underground concourse instead. I didn't know until later that it was because of the falling bodies.

The mood changed in the concourse. People were scrambling now, and not as helpful. It was a different kind of tension. They were no longer escaping death, but running toward freedom. There was even a line outside of Starbucks. I looked at the line like I was watching a movie. While smoking pot… Everything seemed kind of hazy, distant. I just felt numb. My pace was slow.

A hand gripped mine and tugged me forward. It was Henry. "Why the fuck aren't you running?" he said. I didn't know. We only exchanged a few more words before I let him lead me.

We ran for several blocks before the piercing sound of twisting steel and broken concrete cracked through the air as the South Tower began to collapse. I turned and watched. Every fragment of the building. Every wisp of ash. It tumbled down in slow motion while I memorized every detail.

Thick smoke billowed up into the indigo blue sky and carried my memory with it. The shock settled in my chest. I looked up at Henry, who wept. Then there was the blood-curdling scream of a million New Yorkers.

Later that day

I don't know exactly how long I'd been in the hospital before I came to, and the images are still kind of fuzzy. Maybe they always will be. The light from the room entered my eyes in piercing cracks, and the sounds are like broken fragments in my memory. I heard my mother's distant wail, such a gut-wrenching bellow that it's a wonder I ever forgot it; I know I never will again. Henry's face looked down at mine, and he smiled. My eyes closed and when I opened them again, he was gone.

I know now that he made it up. Sometime before I'd fully woken up, when my body was struggling to stay alive and my mind was still discerning what was real and what wasn't, Henry told me a story about a big fight we'd had. It happened after the incident in the alley, he said. I went to his house and yelled at him, told him I hated him when, actually, I loved him. It was believable; love's weird like that. He told me he didn't say it back, that he said he'd be leaving—back to Albuquerque, where he belonged. That he'd no longer be my biggest distraction.

My mind, so vulnerable in this state, believed it had happened for real. In truth, Henry didn't leave because of some dream I had; he left for a fight. He wanted to protect me from the truth. He wanted to be a part of this war. He was the only person who really knew what had happened, and he hid it from me. And now what? I'm supposed to forgive him because he's leaving again? Because his intentions were so noble? *Were they?*

One forgives a thief when they return what is lost. The problem is this: Henry is the thief who stole my memories, but I'm not so sure I wanted them back.

CHAPTER 16

Henry feels like the world's greatest fuck-up. Impulsive Henry, that's him. Same thing he gets in trouble for at work, same thing with women. Why couldn't he keep his fucking mouth shut? Both then and now.

It's true, ya know. He takes what he wants from Emma. Her mind, her body. But he has to. She doesn't know what's good for her, and he can't stop himself from showing her the way—his way. Even if his way isn't any better.

So he wrote her the letter and he gave her the camera. Breaking and entering aside, it's his last good deed. He's hurt her good, but at least it's all in the open now. Emma knows everything, and now she can do whatever she wants. Without him. She's free from him, finally, and yeah, he feels better knowing that. He still feels like shit, but better.

Henry's things are hardly unpacked before he has to pack them again. He'll be back in Georgia tomorrow, then off they go the day after that. Fastest three days ever. Fuck. He should get started now, but he can't seem to pull his ass off this couch. Can't he just sit here and wallow forever?

A knock at the door reminds him he can't.

"Just a minute!"

He slinks off the couch, then pulls his shirt back over his head.

"Emma," he says, opening the door.

She stands. Face red, fists clenched. Henry steps aside and motions for her to come in, but she just stands there frozen-like.

"You can't be that mad at me," he tells her, "or you wouldn't be here now."

Emma is quiet for a long moment, then she seems to relent. Her body relaxes, but just a little.

"You're leaving," she says, meeting his eyes.

"Yeah."

"When?"

"Tomorrow." Silence again. "Will you get in here already?"

Emma steps in slowly. One foot, then another. She stands at the threshold for a long moment before turning to Henry, somehow bright-eyed.

"The patio," she says. "I remember it had a lovely view."

Henry smiles, cupping his hand over hers, then leads her through the living room, the small dining room and then the kitchen, to the patio.

"Where's Tabitha?"

"School," he says.

Emma nods. "Monday, right." She looks out at the street. "I always loved your neighborhood."

"The multi-colored façades," Henry says. "I remember."

"There's so much personality here. I was envious of that,

did you know? When I was gone, I missed it."

"I knew."

The patio is kind of small but extravagant by New York's standards. There's only room for a small but well-built table and two chairs, both padded with comfortable orange cushions. A skinny vase sits on the table between two empty coffee cups. Inside it, a single yellow daisy. Emma sits, then leans over the table to smell it.

"My favorite," she says.

Henry remains standing. "Did you get my letter?"

"Yes."

"We should talk."

Emma nods, smiling. "I know."

"Coffee first?"

"Please."

They don't talk over coffee though. Henry knows better. He picks up the empty mugs and goes back in to brew a pot. When he brings the coffee outside, Emma and Henry sit quietly for ten whole minutes.

She turns to him when she's finished and says, "Why didn't you tell me?"

Henry shrugs. "Would it have mattered?"

"Maybe. Why'd you join, anyway?"

"Duty," he says. "Obligation. Plus I was blazing mad."

"Do you feel better now?"

"No. There is no *feeling better*. I mean, do you?"

"No," she says. "I suppose you're right about that."

"I'm sorry I lied to you, Emma."

"I know…but I understand now. I'm not mad at you."

Not mad. He thinks on this for a moment. Lets the words really settle.

"Thanks," he says. "Do you…"

"What?"

"Never mind. Stop folding your lip."

Emma drops her hand to her lap, then she stands up and paces a little before turning to Henry with her back to the street.

"You must really love me," she tells him.

"I do," he says. "Do you—"

"Yes, Henry. I know that's the thing you were going to ask."

"It is."

She looks away quickly, then back to him. "I wish you weren't leaving."

"Me too."

"Are you afraid?"

"Of what? War?"

"Dying."

"War I'm afraid of," Henry admits. "But I'm not scared to

die."

• • •

It was only mid-morning when Emma and Henry made love again for the second and last time. His room was filled with nice but simple things. A single dresser. A large (and largely empty) closet. An almost-sheer blue curtain, just enough to dull the light. White sheets. Their naked limbs were tangled beneath them.

Henry had taken things slower with her. Really took his time. Was he sorry for what he did before? Was he just savoring? She couldn't tell, nor did she care.

Emma was limp with pleasure, her breath still coming in short gasps, quick and shallow. Her head rested on the firm comfort of his shoulder, and her arm was wedged between their bodies, falling asleep. Her free hand used its fingers to trace his abs and his chest and then cradle his cheek against her palm. They kissed. Their legs were wrapped around each other's, their hearts beating steadily like clocks. One. Two. Three. He held her tightly in his arms.

She felt his tongue on hers, remembering how it had tasted her neck, how it had drawn a masterpiece onto her back, down the length of her spine and the slender curve of her waist, then over her stomach and up to her breasts. She remembered his breath in her ear.

"Tell me why you love me," he'd said.

She smiled. There were a million things she could have told him, but nothing he didn't already know. She loved him for his words, for his mind, for his work. She loved his music. She loved his body and his touch, the way he looked at her when they made love, and even when they didn't. She loved his kindness. She loved his humor. She loved the way he made her feel. She loved him as if their souls were now bonded together, as if he were a part of her own self. And she loved herself—this new self, this person she had now become. She loved him for loving her.

Emma was quiet. She reached for his face and pressed her lips to his, and he didn't ask again.

The day was filled with openness and comfort, with a love so hard and full that Emma knew it would be their last. She savored him, memorized him. She was there to wish him off.

"I'm sorry," he said, seconds before he had to leave.

"For what, Henry?"

"I mean, if I ever got in the way of your dreams, like you said I would. I'm sorry for that."

"Henry," she said, "you are my dreams."

Henry smiled. She let him go.

ONWARD

Ground has broken on the Freedom Tower, what is now officially called One World Trade Center. Construction has been slow, but already the tower, still a skeleton of steel, thrusts up from the lower Manhattan skyline. The windows appear as a sheet of glass around its midsection, but still there is work to be done. Cranes still poke out like antennae from high above the structure. The streets below remain somber, especially today, as the nation continues to heal from its wide open wounds.

For a while, I let him wander freely around. He doesn't really know what he's looking at. He doesn't quite understand what it means. He doesn't know that his grandfather died in this very spot, that his father came to me afterward, and that in the end, because of it all, his father was taken from me too, plucked right from the earth. A life so painfully, fleetingly short.

My sister stands next to me, watching him closely. She's just here for a couple of days, then she'll go back to Oregon where she just started her freshman year at Reed College. Lois is eighteen now, and well past the awkwardness of puberty. The ginger in her hair has faded and she's learned to straighten her frizzy curls, so now it's a sheet of blonde that cascades down her tall, slender frame. Her face is no longer childlike, but that of a woman, with sharp lines and intelligent, wide-set eyes. She stands straight, her head held high as always, but she has not been hardened by her youth. Instead she emits a delicate, graceful sort of beauty.

"Look, Aunt Lo!" His dark tufts of hair flop around as he runs. He spreads his arms out into the wind. "I'm Superman!"

When he gallops toward us, his green eyes brighten and he smiles wide. He stands between Lois and me, reaching for us on either side. I cradle his hand as it melts into mine—into the warm but firm grip of his mother—and in return my heart fills with joy, with love, with achievement, and with pride.

His name is Henry, of course, as I knew it would be from the moment I met him, when his tiny body was first placed in my arms. I knew that's what Henry and my father would have wanted, but more than their wishes, I knew it because that's who he *was*. He had practically declared it himself, that he'd be another strong and handsome Henry who would wiggle his way into my life, into my home and my heart. Another wildly-spirited, beloved Henry who would totally consume me.

As he stands by my side today, everything is clear, all that he is to me. Little Henry is my Freedom Tower, my pool of Reflecting Absence, my own personal monument of marble—perfectly carved, with the names and the memories and the girl from my youth engraved with the finest gold beneath the surface of his skin. He is my treasure, my gift, lifted from the rubble of this great tragedy, thoroughly cleansed of the sands of war.

I think of my grandmother in this moment. She's likely snuggled on the couch next to Charles, watching the ceremony from their farmhouse in Tillamook. I'm certain she's thinking of us too. I remember what she said to me, years ago, before I knew how much it would matter: *One day you may have to find love, and then find love again.*

I think of Henry's mom, too. Her son died quick, a shock that jolted her, perhaps as much as Laura's sudden death had a year earlier. But the pain didn't cause her to wallow and wilt away, or she hid it well. Instead she used her money to travel and show Tabitha the world while maintaining a permanent residence in New York so that young Tabby could have some stability.

I took her place as co-owner of the studio (where Chloe is manning the fort today) forgoing my audition with Juilliard. At nearly six months pregnant, I wouldn't have had a choice, but it's not a choice I would have made anyway. It's not the institution that I love; it's the dance. It has always been the dance. Teaching at the studio gives me a fulfillment I know Juilliard never could.

The ceremony begins with a calm that washes over the clusters of people gathered around. Henry's squirmy little hand grips mine, and he tugs me toward him.

"What about Nana?" he asks. "And cousin Tabby Tat?"

"We'll see them after," I tell him.

"And then we go on the boat?" His eyes are pleading, but I know he has nothing to worry about. The plans for today haven't changed.

"Yes, Henry. Then we go on the boat."

"To see the lady, right momma?"

"Of course."

I lift him up to my hip so he can see. He's almost getting too big to be held like this anymore. Restlessly, he shuffles himself around. His impatience is swelling; I can tell by the way he raises his voice at me, making sure I can hear him above the music and the rustle of the crowds.

"Tabby Tat says she never ever saw her yet!"

"Shhh," I whisper, inching him up higher, to my waist. "I know."

In response, he squeezes his lips together with two tiny fingers.

"Is it the beginning now?" he asks in a sweet, quiet voice, leaning his face in close to my ear. This time, I can hardly hear him.

"Yes, Henry," I tell him. "It's the beginning now."

ACKNOWELEDGEMENTS

This novel is the product of over two years of writing and a wealth of support from fellow authors and friends. I am tremendously indebted to all of my critiquers and beta readers. In no particular order, thank you Gracey Mullins, Candance Moore, Rachel Cross, Henry McCulloch, John Kang, Kimberly Sullivan, R. Ellis Novak, Rachelle Ayala, Rich Marcello, M.J. Ascot, NJ Layouni, Faith M. Coppola, Carroll Sullivan, Cesar Gonzalez, Cecily Loring, Ashlinn Craven, and Critique Circle members Turnstiles, Hijo, Mariaxuxas, Ssjohnson, Etyrrell, and Jeaniekate. A special thanks to CC's "FictionDog," my dear friend and very first peer-critiquer. This book would not be what it is without your intelligent critiques and unequaled encouragement of my writing.

There are many more fellow writers who contributed their feedback to various sections of this novel, and I thank you so much!

To my loving family, thank you all. You have fostered my writing and believed in me from the start, even after reading my earliest stuff (so embarrassing). I would not have gotten this far without your support, and I am forever grateful.

Gustavo Dias, thank you for your generous feedback, for being my go-to expert on all things Army-related, and for supporting my writing in its infancy.

Thanks to my valiant proofreader and incredible friend Stephany Renfrow, and to my cover artist Clarissa Yeo—for "catching the vision" of *After Henry* and for being so willing to partner with me on my most ambitious project.

Lastly, thank you Jeremy, for your love and encouragement. For inspiring me and for sharing your knowledge. When finishing a novel felt like climbing Mount Everest and I wanted to bail, thank you for giving me the swift kick in the butt I needed to move forward. You've created a fighter, ya know. My bailing days are over.

ABOUT THE AUTHOR

After graduating from the University of Central Florida in 2009 with a degree in Communications, Michelle Josette moved to Dallas, Texas, where she is now living her dream as a freelance writer and editor. *After Henry* is her first novel.

To learn more about Michelle, including her editing services and upcoming books, visit her website at mjbookeditor.com.

Made in the USA
San Bernardino, CA
21 October 2014